BE A
SUPER SALESPERSON

Cyrus M Gonda | Dr. Kalim Khan

BE A
SUPER SALESPERSON

Cyrus M Gonda | Dr. Kalim Khan

EMBASSY BOOKS
www.embassybooks.in

Published in India by :
EMBASSY BOOK DISTRIBUTORS
120, Great Western Building,
Maharashtra Chamber of Commerce Lane,
Fort, Mumbai - 400 023.
Tel : (+91-22) 22819546 / 32967415
Email : info@embassybooks.in
Website: www.embassybooks.in

ISBN 13: 978-93-80227-63-4

Dedication

Deeba, this one for you. Thanks for being there, for bearing , for caring and for helping make each endeavor possible. Words can never express what I owe you in life.

Dr. Kalim Khan

To my mum and papa, who mean everything to me. Thanks for everything.

Cyrus M Gonda

Contents

Acknowledgements — ix

Foreword — xi

Preface — xiii

1. The Flight — 1
2. Perseverance — 7
3. Eye for Detail — 13
4. Power of a Smile — 19
5. Glory of Grooming — 23
6. Communication - The Key — 29
7. Effective Listening — 35
8. Honour Commitment — 41
9. Punctuality Wins — 47
10. Love your Brand — 53
11. Knowledge of Profession — 57
12. Positive Attitude — 63
13. Go the Extra Mile — 71
14. Analyse Data — 77
15. Give More than You Get — 85
16. Team Work — 91
17. Respect your Competitors — 99
18. Customise your Offerings — 105
19. Accept Rejection — 111
20. Practice Persistence — 117

21.	Develop Speed of Mind	123
22.	Avoid Prejudice	129
23.	Understand your Customer	135
24.	Focus on After Sales Service	141
25.	Develop Relationships	147
26.	Value Moments of Truth	153
27.	Generate Positive Word of Mouth	159
28.	Success through Networking	165
29.	Value over Price	173
30.	Aim for Excellence	179
31.	Escalate Feedback	187
32.	Holistic Selling	193

| **Checklists for Fail-proof Selling** | **199** |
| **Song of the Super Salesperson** | **219** |

Acknowledgements

When it comes to thanking for all the riches and bounty
Our heads shall always bow down to the blessings of the
Almighty

Forever we shall be indebted to friends and their support
It is to them we owe our success card of report

Can never thank or repay the love of all our students
They are and forever in our hearts as residents

There are some efforts of special people that can never be repaid
Words fall short to express gratitude to you Osaid

Your association has been value adding and enriching
A special thanks to all who have been a part of our consulting
and training

To appreciate your support that is indeed our duty
Thanks are due to the Rizvi staff and faculty

Cyrus says a big thank to our parents for being the guiding stars
of our life
And Kalim adds besides them another special thanks for his
wife

Foreword

As such, sales is the raison d'etre for any organisation / product / brand . . . This is a known fact. But the challenge for any salesperson, in a hyper-competitive world, is no longer limited to merely pushing their products; instead, the art of selling now lies in identifying unarticulated consumer needs and developing a "saleable story" that promotes your brand / product as the solution provider to that need. It is needless to say that post-consumption experience should match with the pre-sale story for any sustainable re-purchase.

A salesperson today must learn from the principles of a "Phoenix" – a mythical bird that never dies. The Phoenix flies far ahead to the front, always scanning the landscape and distant space. It has the capacity for vision, for collecting sensory information about the environment and the events unfolding within it. Similarly, like the Phoenix, the salesperson of today must soar ahead of his times, envision the unfolding and dynamic world, utilise these inputs to foster "creative disruption", which in turn would help unlock new success formulae and sales strategies that create unique value propositions for the organisation as well as for customers.

And all of this is done "in flight", i.e. from a sales perspective, while the salesperson is in discussion with customers . . . there is no time to come back, think, ideate and revert . . . So, solutions need to be developed 'then and there'. As such, the salesperson in this dynamic age needs to evolve beyond mere numbers into a more holistic business approach which involve issues of future sustainability, implications on ethics, regulatory compliances. All in all, it is the era of a "Super Salesperson".

"When the winds of change blow, some people build walls while others build windmills . . ." Well, the life of a salesperson definitely has undergone a sea of change. What needs to be seen is whether the salesperson will build walls to protect his old ways of selling or will he harness the force of the wind to take off like the flight of the phoenix. The very fact that YOU have bought this book goes to show that YOU want to know how to build windmills and that's a great start ...

Regards,

Joy Chakraborthy
Chief Revenue Officer & Head Niche Channels
Zee Entertainment Enterprises Ltd.

Preface

Organisations today perform hundreds of diverse activities.

But out of these hundreds of activities, there is only one activity that generates revenue. And that is the activity of **SELLING**.

All other activities are costs to the organisation.

And hence it is mandatory for any individual contemplating a rosy career in marketing, to have a worthwhile exposure in sales and be equipped with high degrees of selling skills. We believe that a person has no rights to spend even a single penny until he has earned it for himself. The problem with young recruits entering Corporate India today is that they straightaway want to enter the marketing domain without going through the school of the sales function. Our reservations are that most of these individuals:

- Have not understood the difference between sales and marketing
- Have always looked down upon sales as a profession while choosing career a option
- Are poorly or inadequately equipped with selling skills

Such a set of individuals in any function, lacking fundamental grass-root knowledge and awareness have always caused colossal damage to their organisation

'Earn to spend' : is our philosophy, and the rationale of this book.

This book is an attempt to equip all budding sales and marketing professionals with the absolutely necessary ingredients of perfect selling skills.

The Song of the Super Salesperson is made up of thirty two couplets, each comprising an indispensable attribute or philosophy that shall ensure success in sales and marketing functions in specific, and for the organisation in general.

A decade of research, soul-searching and dialogues with practitioners, experts, and front-line sales staff across industries has helped us develop an exhaustive, all inclusive set of thirty two attributes which are a mandatory must for any individual to succeed in the sales and marketing profession.

Our challenge and assurance therefore is that, if these thirty two attributes are in place and are practiced holistically, there is nothing that a sales and marketing person should lack to achieve success in selling.

Further, the book also contains a well researched and comprehensive set of eleven highly practical check-lists that have been developed by us to facilitate fool-proofing in the selling function.

The thirty two couplets are our contribution for enabling **Kaizen** (the Japanese concept of Continuous Improvement) in selling and the set of check-lists is our assurance of **Poka-Yoke** (the Japanese concept of mistake-proofing) in selling.

If we are permitted, and before you commence reading, a few words of advice. These thirty two attributes will work. They shall work. But the pre-requisite of **enjoying** the function of selling is something that only you as an individual can get to the table. So enjoy your job and succeed in it. Keep singing the Song of the Super Salesperson and equip yourself with the Super Salesperson's Skill Set which this book gifts you with for a lifetime success in selling.

Happy Reading

Cyrus M Gonda
Dr. Kalim Khan

1

Ever onward, ever upward,
your only goal is to reach the sky

Ever onward, ever upward,
you can reach it if you try

The old and true saying goes – **If you aim for the stars, you reach the moon.**

The direction for sales success lies true when your focus is constantly in the onward and upward direction. Always.

Have you ever tried balancing a stick on the tip of your forefinger and attempted to keep that stick upright and steady? Try it. It is possible. But **ONLY** if you keep your gaze firmly fixed on the top end of the stick. The moment you shift your gaze to your finger (on which the bottom part of the stick rests), the stick will topple over.

Aim at perfection in everything, though in most things it is unattainable. They who aim at it and persevere, will come much nearer to it than those whose laziness makes them give it up as unattainable.

\- Lord Chesterfield

Each of us in the field of selling has to aim onward and upward. The objective is for **ALL** of us involved in the great profession of selling to evolve into great salespersons.

There is no contest.

There is no such thing as – **'Only a few can achieve greatness.'**

We **ALL** have it within ourselves to succeed. Persistence is the key. We move onward by constantly putting one foot in front of the other, never ceasing or halting in our effort.

Each of us aspiring for success in the selling profession has to identify a single, common direction in which to proceed. Onward and upward lies that road. There is no other way to go.

People who are unable to motivate themselves must be content with mediocrity, no matter how impressive their other talents.

- Andrew Carnegie

Striving to become a well loved and a well respected salesperson ought to be your primary goal. It is not that monetary goals are not important.

They are very important indeed. In today's world, one cannot survive on love and fresh air.

But our message is, that once the primary goal that we have outlined is achieved, **ALL** other professional goals; monetary and otherwise, will automatically fall into place.

Not failure, but low aim, is a crime.

- James Russell Lowell

In 1942, Rafael Solano sat on a boulder in a dry river bed, thoroughly exhausted. He had been searching for diamonds along with his companions in Venezuela. He picked up a pebble and announced to his friends that he felt this was the 999, 999th pebble he had picked up, without finding a single diamond. He was now quitting. A friend urged him – "Pick up one more stone and make it a million."

To please his friend, Solano agreed, and picked up a stone about the size of a hen's egg. It was a diamond. And what a diamond it was. A New York diamond dealer paid Solano $200,000 (way back in 1942), for that millionth 'pebble'. The stone was named the 'Liberator', and till date is the largest and purest diamond ever found. It could still have been lying unclaimed on a Venezuelan river bed if Solano hadn't made that one last attempt.

Confidence and enthusiasm are the greatest sales producers in any kind of economy.

\- O B Smith

Another related aspect that average salespersons attempting to transform themselves into Super Salespersons need to focus on, is to avoid the temptation and the tendency to choose the easier product to sell, or the easier territory to harvest. The salespersons who have made it big; who are role models of success for the rest of us to follow, have honed and sharpened their selling skills by deliberately selecting to work with the most demanding clients and in the most difficult territories. That is the way to perfect and sharpen your selling skills.

It is better to aim at perfection and miss, than to aim at imperfection and hit it.

\- Thomas J Watson

A professor once devised a test for his senior college students, who were soon to graduate and go into the corporate world.

The questions in the test he had devised were divided into three categories, and the students were allowed to select questions to attempt from any one category of their choice.

- The questions in the first category were the toughest, and worth a hundred points each if the students got them right
- The second category contained easier questions, which were worth fifty points each
- The third category contained the simplest questions, each worth twenty points

Once the students chose their categories and attempted the test, the scores were declared.

- The students who had selected the category with the toughest questions received an **'A'** grade, even if most of their answers were wrong
- The students who had chosen the second category all received a **'B'** grade
- And the students who chose the simplest questions were awarded a **'C'** grade, even if they had got all their answers correct

The students who received a **'B'** and a **'C'** grade were unhappy with the marking pattern and asked the professor for an explanation.

The professor smiled and replied – **"I wasn't testing your book knowledge. I was testing your aim."**

Anyone who doesn't know what it means to have painful feet doesn't know what selling is.
- Alfred Heineken

The Brains Trust Pearl:
Aim High. Look back not to repent, but look back only to learn from past mistakes.

2

Remember that Rome
wasn't built in half a day

Work honest, work hard, and
things will have to go your way

The words – '**honesty**' and '**hard-work**' go hand-in-hand when it comes to success in selling.

The idea is to make sure not to cut corners or take short cuts. These can only lead to haphazard and unpredictable outcomes. We're sure that's not your goal, is it? Often, an eye on short-term success and the zeal to achieve immediate targets tends to take people far away from their ultimate goal. This will also result in such persons using means, methods and practices, which although may have become a norm today, are out-rightly damaging for any career, including selling.

We have often heard this line – '**I don't know how, and neither do I care how you achieve the results, but I want you to get them.**'

There cannot be **ANY** statement more degrading and demeaning in the profession of sales. Such statements originating from the top, inevitably result in selling practices which are not only unethical, but also non-methodical and non-systematic. In such scenarios, everyone ultimately loses.

> *All human errors have their root in impatience; in a premature breaking off of methodical procedure.*
>
> - Franz Kafka

One thing that you as a salesperson need to avoid at all cost, is being haphazard in your approach to selling.

Rather, develop and follow a systematic approach to your selling process, which will inculcate in you the '**Super Salesperson's Skill Set**,' which is the purpose of the '**Song of the Super Salesperson.**'

Please do **NOT** skip the essential and necessary steps in the selling and relationship building process, which we have enumerated in future couplets, in detail, with clear examples.

A systematic approach is essential for success in a sales career. Always.

Setting up your systems may take you a little time, but once your systems are in place, they ensure you of a smooth ride with no speed-breakers or hindrances.

Honesty and **hard-work** is the key.

As far as **hard-work** is concerned, do **NOT** get into the habit of completing your five mandatory sales calls a day as soon as you can and then rushing home for an afternoon nap. No salesperson ever made it big this way.

And as far as **honesty** goes, it is incorrect to assume that '**nice guys finish last.**'

> *What is important to remember is that NICE GUYS ALWAYS FINISH.*
>
> - Cyrus M Gonda, Dr. Kalim Khan

Unlike their dishonest counterparts, nice guys are **NEVER** disqualified from the race half-way through by their customers for following unethical practices.

When it comes to the matter of integrity in sales, honesty is always at a premium.

- Honesty to your customer
- Honesty to the organisation that you represent and which provides you with your livelihood
- Honesty to your boss
- Honesty to your own conscience

Robert Cialdini, a popular professor of psychology and a reputed author, gives the example of an honest mechanic who gave him an estimate of $45 for repairs on his car. Another mechanic had previously quoted an estimate of $500 for the same work. Cialdini, who owns many cars, and has a huge network of wealthy friends, has retained the honest mechanic for life, as well as recommended him to all his friends. This honest mechanic earned far, far more than a mere one-time con-man's fee of $500.

Remember, most customers today take a second and even a third opinion.

- Cyrus M Gonda, Dr. Kalim Khan

We know of a mid-sized company, which along with many others, bid for a contract that a giant conglomerate had put out.

In the midst of the bidding process, this mid-sized bidder realised that it did not possess the capacity and resources to carry out a timely and quality completion of the said project, and requested permission to back out of the bidding.

This was partly due to the fact that in the meanwhile they had diverted some of their resources onto another project they had been awarded.

The representatives of the conglomerate asked the reason for the intermittent backing out.

The bidding organisation honestly replied that they did not want to commit to a project if they were not comfortable in guaranteeing the completion to the client's full satisfaction.

The representatives of the conglomerate were so impressed with this honesty and transparency, that on the spot, they offered eight smaller subsequent projects scheduled for the next financial year to this mid-sized firm without an afterthought.

Remember, even a crook would prefer an honest man to work for him.

- Cyrus M Gonda, Dr. Kalim Khan

Sam Rayburn, the legendary Speaker of the United States' House of Representatives, was once asked in an interview – "Mr. Speaker, you see probably a hundred people a day. You tell each one 'Yes', or 'No', or 'Maybe'. You are never seen taking notes on what you told them, but I have never heard of you forgetting what you promised them. What is your secret?"

Rayburn's answer is an exemplary lesson for all salespersons. **"If you tell the truth the first time, you don't need to remember what you told them when you first met them."**

The Brains Trust Pearl:
Honest, hard work wins the day, every day.

3

Do not merely fix your mind
upon the quickness and the pace

It is always steady, sure and perfect,
that wins the long race

'Speed Kills' – Reads a slogan on a Tee-Shirt.

In today's fast paced world, the gentle tortoise may be an endangered species.

But the super-fast cheetah and the speedy tiger are rapidly moving towards extinction themselves.

Man today is the master of Planet Earth, not due to his physical strength, but thanks to his curiosity, intellect and willingness to learn and to constantly improve in every arena of his activity.

It is this thirst for improvement and perfection in all spheres of functioning that thrusts mankind onward, enabling him to survive and thrive in the remotest and the most inhospitable of environments.

In a speeding car, it is not possible to observe, assimilate, understand and enjoy the surrounding landscape and environment, and absorb the details of nature's beauty.

Similarly, a salesperson who is always in a hurry, always on the run, **loses out on important details** which a steadier salesman would observe, absorb and benefit from.

An eye for the minutest detail, which some may consider unimportant, is what makes all the difference to your sales performance, and ultimately leads to a delighted customer.

An eye for the minutest detail leads to accuracy in understanding your customer's unique needs and fulfilling them to the best of your ability by customising your product and service offering.

Eye-for-detail is a much more crucial factor in attaining sales success, than is mere haste.

\- Cyrus M Gonda, Dr. Kalim Khan

An eye-for-detail is the hallmark of the professional in every field. It sets apart the successful professionals and puts them many levels above the amateurs.

As one example, an amateur hunter who is hunting in snowy conditions, and who camouflages himself by wearing white clothing, can still be observed by his prey, which can see the cold breath emanating from the hunter's mouth. So the experienced hunter puts some snow in his mouth, which prevents icy breath from releasing. A fantastic example of developing an eye-for-detail and attaining the objective.

Similarly, every profession (including sales), has its finer points, which the experts and the true professionals make constant and systematic efforts to learn and practice. **Understanding and implementing these finer points mark the dividing line between the amateur and the professional.**

Become a sales professional who strives for perfection.

Do not sacrifice 'Eye-for-Detail' at the altar of 'haste'. Both CANNOT co-exist.

- Cyrus M Gonda, Dr. Kalim Khan

No gold medals are ever awarded for running a fast race in the wrong direction. Business is not only about making money. It is about making money consistently.

Consistency is the result that flows from perfection.

Perfection results when proper planning is done to the highest possible degree. As a salesperson, you need to spend the maximum time in sharpening your axe. The fable of sharpening the axe is well worth repeating for the benefit of all salespersons.

Two woodcutters went to a forest to chop a tree. One woodcutter immediately rushed to a nearby tree and started hitting away with his axe. Many powerful blows later, a lot of energy expended, he sat down exhausted, with little result to show for all his hard work. His friend, who had patiently invested some time in sharpening his axe, selected a strong tree, gave two swift blows, and the tree was down.

This clearly demonstrates that achieving your objective with perfection requires proper planning.

SPEED comes in a poor third place after PERFECTION and CONSISTENCY.

- Cyrus M Gonda, Dr. Kalim Khan

If you as a salesperson are **perfect** in your work, (that is, you are error free), and you are also **consistently perfect**, (which means that **every** time you sell and serve, you are error free), then the speed of your work will automatically occur as a by-product.

Focus on perfection and consistency, and speed will be your bonus reward.

Practice doesn't make perfect. Perfect practice makes perfect.

- Vince Lombardi

In sales, the key word is – **Cultivate**.

As Sam Lewis said – 'I feel like a gardener who planted a bunch of seeds and nothing came up: and again the next year he planted a bunch of more seeds and nothing came up; and again the next year planted more seeds with the same result, and so on and on and on. And then this year he planted a bunch of seeds; not only did they all come up, but all the seeds from the previous year came up and all the seeds from the years before and so on. Now I'm running around harvesting all the crops.'

A friend of ours, who is already a successful entrepreneur, mentioned to us that he was keeping in regular touch with all his college batch-mates. He says – "I've planted my seeds well. Soon all my friends will be reaching decision making positions in their organisations. The seeds are ripening. Now I'll reap the fruits."

A word of caution.

When we say **steady**, we don't mean **sluggish**.

We rather refer to a kind of steady which was explained to us at meal times when we were young.

Chew your food thirty two times before swallowing' – is what we were told.

There is a wealth of meaning in this. In fact, there is a best-selling book and programme on the subject of weight reduction that assures weight loss, and the essence of it can be summed up in two words – **'CHEW SLOWLY'**.

Perfection is a road, not a destination. Every time I live,
I get an education.

- Burk Hudson

The Brains Trust Pearl:
Develop a keen eye for detail and a burning thirst for perfection in every area which is of importance to your customer.

4

**Be happy, joyous, cheerful;
always let your heart rejoice**

**Between a smile and a frown,
by far the smile's the better choice**

A wise man once said – "You're never fully dressed till you've put on a **BIIIG BRIGHT SMILE."**

A big, bright, natural, genuine smile is positively infectious.

The smile does you and all around you a world of good.

To succeed in the selling profession, you need to constantly strive to keep your personal energy levels high.

You should be truly thankful that you have an opportunity to earn an honest living and support yourself and your family.

When you stand in front of your customer, the personal energy levels you summon from within yourself, will greatly help you as well as your customer to have belief and confidence in the brand that you represent.

A prospective employer would prefer to hire a cheerful employee. A prospective customer would prefer to deal with a cheerful salesperson.

- Cyrus M Gonda, Dr. Kalim Khan

The only difference that exists in you between the times that you felt charged up, as compared to the times you felt droopy and down, are your personal energy levels and attitude at those different moments of time.

An **optimist** goes to the window each morning and says –
"Good morning, God."

A **pessimist** goes to the window each morning and says –
"Good God, morning."

Positive thinking coupled with positive actions put you past the victory line in sales as well as in life.

- Cyrus M Gonda, Dr. Kalim Khan

There is a beautiful story about a little orphan child, who had no family, and no one to look after her or love her.

One day, when she was feeling exceptionally sad and alone, she noticed a poor butterfly caught in a thorny bush. The more the butterfly struggled to free itself, the deeper the thorns sank into its fragile body. The girl took pity on it, and carefully released the creature from the thorns. Instead of flying away, the butterfly transformed before the little girl's eyes into a beautiful fairy. The young girl stared in disbelief.

The fairy told the girl – "For your act of kindness, I will grant you any wish you would like."

The little girl thought and replied – "I want to be happy always."

The fairy whispered the secret of everlasting happiness in the girl's ear and flew away.

Years passed. The little girl grew up, and no one in the land was as happy as she. All asked her the secret of her state of happiness, but she merely smiled and replied – "The secret of my happiness is that I listened to a good fairy when I was a little girl."

When she grew very old and was on her deathbed (still happy), the neighbours gathered around her and were afraid her wonderful secret of happiness would be lost when she passed on. They begged her to tell them the secret before it would be lost forever.

The lovely old lady smiled and replied – "The fairy told me that everyone, no matter how secure they seemed, no matter how young or old, how rich or poor, **HAD NEED OF ME**. Helping them would keep me happy."

A busy day is a happy day.

- Unknown

The message for all Super Salespersons is clear – **ALL YOUR CUSTOMERS ARE IN NEED OF YOU.**

If they **DIDN'T** need you, they wouldn't **BE** your customers in the first place, would they?

So don't look at going out of the way to help a customer with a unique need as an unpleasant task.

Don't make a sulky face. Do it willingly and cheerfully.

In fact these are the very occasions and opportunities you should wait for and grab, as fulfilling these requests define your supreme success as a Super Salesperson.

> *I don't know what your destiny will be, but one thing I know; the ones among you who will be really happy are those who have sought and found how to serve.*
> - Dr. Albert Schweitzer

The following survey findings would surely bring an immediate smile to your face:

- In a university study of sports teams, it was found that the more optimistic the team members on the whole, the better they performed and the more successful they were
- Another study showed that those who were considered as optimists at age 25, led healthier lives in later age, while pessimists more often had health problems later on in life

> *The most wasted of all days is that during which one has not laughed.*
> - Sebastien Chamfort

The Brains Trust Pearl:
Radiate genuine joy and cheer from every pore of your being.

5

Wouldst you better your chance of selling,
to your prospect you should be appealing

Improve your grooming, perfect grooming;
this will make for better dealing

This is one of the simplest tasks that a salesperson can perform to increase his productivity many times over. Unfortunately, because it is so simple, it is often ignored.

Take the armed forces personnel as your role model for grooming. They are clean shaven and have shining, polished shoes even on their day off. It's a habit with them. Make it a habit with you.

The following are a few basic grooming tips which we have found would do salespersons a world of good:

- Well trimmed hair and a clean shaven face do not require Herculean efforts. So trim your hair neatly and regularly, and you can't go wrong

- A clean shaven face makes you look fresh and at your best. Else the attention of your prospect will be on your stubble. Surveys prove that a clean shaven look is one of the most attractive features a man can possess, and this look is totally within your control

- You don't need to be blessed with model features to be a super success in the sales profession. But you definitely do need to be well groomed and presentable. This will make you a charming person to deal with

- Another feature which is always noticed is your nails. Whether it is while you are shaking hands with your prospect, or while using hand gestures during your presentation. Dirt under nails and uncut, long nails are not an appealing sight

- Ice is the magic touch for glowing facial skin. Apply some ice on your facial skin every night. We all know how refreshing a cold towel on our face feels

- Drink a lot of water. Water is great for your skin. Drinking more water also makes you less liable to stuff yourself with junk food

Groom yourself each morning for a beautiful and profitable day.

Before you positively project your product or your service to your prospect, you first have to positively project yourself as a well groomed individual.

- Cyrus M Gonda, Dr. Kalim Khan

A brilliant example of the power of grooming in the sales profession would be that of an MBA student of ours. After passing out, like many other fresh MBAs, he joined the sales department of a private bank. Unlike many others, he gave great importance to his personal grooming, right from day one of his career.

This lad made a few wise investments the moment he started working. He got stitched for himself three well fitting suits, purchased a few excellent ties, as well as two good pairs of formal shoes. Each day that he came to work; he came attired in a suit. His colleagues laughed and even sometimes mocked, as they themselves never wore a suit to office. Our student smiled and took all this teasing in his stride. When his colleagues went on sales calls, they traveled by public transport and pocketed the taxi fare to which they were entitled. Our student went on his sales calls by taxi, honestly using the taxi allowance the office provided. As a result, he reached his client's location well before time, looking fresh and smelling good, having used a deodorant in the taxi on the way.

Within his first two months on job, his sales volumes showed a superior performance as compared to his colleagues. Appointments which were impossible to secure for other salespersons, were secured by our student with ease. Personal secretaries of those bosses who wouldn't give a glance to the averagely groomed salesperson, willingly gave appointments to this fine lad.

One fine day, the sales manager of his bank secured an important appointment with the senior management team of a potential client organisation. He wanted one of his sales officers to accompany him for this meeting.

Can you guess whom did he select?

You're right. Our student .And can you guess **why** was he the one selected?

Right again. And all due to the attention this lad paid to his grooming.

The icing on the cake was, that in this particular client meet where his boss took him along, the clients initially felt that our student was the boss, (due to his impeccable dress), and greeted him first. The actual boss was initially sidelined.

Remember, clothes need not be expensive to be tasteful.

Let a friend who is well versed in corporate attire accompany you on your shopping rounds.

We would also like to quote another incident where a particular H R manager of an organisation severely reprimanded two young management trainees from the sales department who were hardly a month old in the organisation. In fact the reprimand was so severe, and the disciplinary action taken so stringent, that it was a wake-up call for the entire batch of management trainees who had been recruited that year.

One rainy day, these two trainees had just entered office, and they met their H R manager on their way to their seats. The H R manager, who had been with this organisation since long, and had a keen eye for minute detail, saw these trainees and asked them where they had been since morning. In a show of one-upmanship, the trainees proudly announced that they had been for a meeting with a key account.

It was then that the H R manager lost her cool and lambasted these sales trainees in front of the entire office. These kids had put on **plastic rainy-wear shoes** (it being monsoon time), which were shoddy and shabby looking. For some of you this may sound trivial, and also perhaps the sensible thing to do during the monsoon.

But the H R lady had a point of view which we very strongly endorse and support. While reprimanding these sales trainees, she constantly made it clear that the hefty salary structure given to them had a good reason behind it. It permitted them to groom and dress themselves to display to clients that the company took good care of its staff, and furthermore, when they were on a client call, they were not representing themselves, as much as they were representing the organisation. Hence it was mandatory that these sales trainees dress up and present themselves in a manner that befit the stature of the employing organisation.

It is **NOT** about the plastic rainy-wear shoes. It is about a message, that even the most apparently insignificant component of dress and attire matters, and matters big-time.

A wonderful case in point is the dress-code, display and discipline at all points in time maintained by the representatives of the armed forces. It is their perfect grooming, (even if it is white attire, which by default in their case is spotless), which is a clear indicator of their control over all situations at all times.

Another important aspect of grooming and appearance a salesperson should give importance to, is that of physical well-being, which ensures that along with the best of clothes, one is in good shape to carry them off to best advantage.

We strongly advocate that you take up a particular sport you enjoy, or invest a few hours every week in a gym, which is sufficient to get any individual into reasonable shape.

A healthy and well groomed exterior will generate self-confidence to face the most demanding customer.

A salesman is someone with a smile on his face and a shine on his shoes.

- George Gobel

The Brains Trust Pearl:
Good grooming opens closed doors.

6

Gentle walking, gentle talking,
make a perfect gentleman

None can then ever resist you,
though he tries the best he can

The skill of being an effective communicator is a very powerful tool that a salesperson needs to develop and maintain in order to be successful.

Effective communication is not only about a vast vocabulary, an American accent, and verbal glory.

Effective communication has more to do with **WHEN** to speak and **WHAT** to speak. It takes us three years to learn to speak, but it takes a lifetime to learn when to speak and what to speak.

You may not mind losing business to a competitor on a technical issue. That could be due to his product or service being more suitable to the customer's needs. That is a factor which is outside your control.

But you would **DEFINITELY** find it hard to accept that you lost a sale due to a communication or etiquette failure at your end. This is something which you could so easily have taken care of.

Correct etiquette, impeccable manners and a pleasing tone are all essential to sales success, and encompass the definition of the term **– Gentleman.**

Practice:

- The correct walk
- The right hand-shake
- The proper way to give and receive a visiting card

Always speak in a pleasing tone. If your tone of voice is naturally harsh, do not use that as an excuse. Overcome it through practice. It can be done. Many have overcome this apparent handicap. A sweet sounding tone of voice works miracles. As the song from the famous musical, **Mary Poppins,** goes:

'A spoonful of sugar helps the medicine go down, in the most delightful way'

We mentioned in the previous couplet that the right grooming is important. Clothes definitely make the man.

But what is equally, if not more important than your attire, is the way that you carry yourself and the way that you speak.

We are all instantly attracted to some persons by their positive body language and their manner of speaking. These persons have not been born or blessed with these qualities. They have worked hard to acquire them.

We recently met a former MBA student of ours, who is now employed with the sales department of a leading credit card company. Her profile involves the selling of credit cards to corporate and individual clientele. We asked her how the job was going. As she had specialised in Marketing and not in Finance during her MBA, we enquired whether she had any difficulty in understanding the technical nuances or the financial aspects of the product she was selling. Her reply surprised us.

She said – "Sir, it is **ONLY** about communication. Believe me, when I meet a prospect, the manner in which I present my product, which is dependent upon my ability to communicate in a pleasing manner, is the single most important parameter responsible for my success."

We are in no way implying that a successful salesperson can ignore or overlook the other parameters we have identified as important. But today, clear and pleasing communication appears to be around the top of the wish list of attributes for a successful salesperson to possess.

We have heard of many software and finance persons being sent by their organisations on deputation overseas. They are selected to represent their organisations in Western countries due to their technical expertise. Although they are deputed for a period of around two to three years, we observe that many of them return within a few weeks of reaching there.

The reason for their hasty return, in most cases, is that they are unable to:

- Adjust to the social environment
- To make pleasant small talk
- To have the right dining etiquette

A public sector bank, for which we conduct Customer Service and Sales Training workshops, has rightly realised the supreme importance these areas have on business outcomes, as an increasing volume of their clients belong to an NRI background.

These clients have traveled abroad, and have been exposed to a Five Star culture and environment. These clients prefer to interact with staff and salespersons who display the right social awareness, table manners and general etiquette. These clients observe whether you are polite and kind to the waiting staff. They observe all this and much more.

This bank decided to conduct training programmes for its staff in the area of dining etiquette, as a lot of their business with their key clients was finalised over dinner. In the programme, we:

- Explained to the staff the finer points of the table arrangement
- Made them practice dining with the right cutlery
- Ensured they correctly identified which forks, knives and spoons were to be used during which part of the meal
- Trained them not to let the cutlery play a symphony on the plate during dinner

And this training worked wonders in improving the confidence and the soft skills of the employees, which ultimately translated into superior customer interactions, more sales, and ultimately higher profitability for the bank.

The business dinner is **NOT** just about the food. A business dinner is a unique opportunity for the salesperson to create an overall positive impact on the client.

Etiquette and correct communication are definitely skills which can be acquired and perfected through practice. Don't let a lack of them be a stumbling block for your sales career.

Be a craftsman and gentle in your speech so that thou may be strong; for the strength of a person is his tongue, and speech is mightier than all fighting.

\- Maxims of Ptahhotep

The Brains Trust Pearl:

Develop pleasing manners and sweet speech. This does NOT mean indulging in blatant and insincere flattery..

7

Personalised service is what your customers prefer,
customised service is what your customers need

So let your customers do the talking,
your job is to listen and do the deed

Don't you wish you possessed a magic wand which would help you to know exactly what was going on in the minds of your prospects and your customers?

Well, fortunately you **DO** have such a wand.

Or rather, you **CAN** acquire one. A very effective wand. And all for free.

The name of this magic wand is – **Listening.**

All salespersons need to develop the quality known as listening.

What most of us are good at is **hearing**. To be good at hearing, all that one needs is a good, functioning pair of ears. **Hearing is nothing but the sound waves massaging your ear-drums.**

Listening is a totally different ball-game altogether.

LISTENING.

That's what this magic wand is called.

Listening is not an activity that involves only the ears.

> *True listening involves ears, eyes, heart, body,*
> *mind and soul.*
>
> - Cyrus M Gonda, Dr. Kalim Khan

Many successful managers, when asked what special skills they possessed which helped them reach the very top of their business hierarchy, mentioned that the skill they felt which was most responsible for their success was good listening.

Most salespersons make the mistake of speaking too much about themselves and the organisation they represent.

Ideally, the maximum time during the sales interaction or presentation should be invested (the correct word is invested, and not spent), in listening to what your customer has to say.

You never learn anything while you are speaking. You only learn while you're listening.

- Unknown

That's what we said the magic wand is all about. It helps you to learn what is going on in your customer's mind.

The word LISTEN and the word SILENT are made up of the same letters of the alphabet.

We were recently revamping the computer laboratory in our college, and were identifying a vendor for the job. It was a huge project, and we wanted to get the job done by the person who would first and foremost understand our unique needs in the best possible manner. Most of the salespersons who came to meet us to represent their firm for meeting our needs, spent almost all their presentation time speaking about their goodness and what they felt they could provide us. We politely heard them out. The **ONE** salesperson who impressed us the most (and who ultimately got our business), was the one who first asked us intelligent questions regarding our specific and unique requirements, and then kept silent and listened intently when we (the customers), spoke.

A wonderful folk tale in the words of **Qushayri** follows.

A ruler cared for one of his servants above all others. The others were envious of this favourite, and wondered why he was the chosen one. One day, when the ruler was out riding with all his servants, they saw in the distance a snow capped mountain. The ruler stopped, gazed at the snow covered peak, and bowed his head. The favourite servant immediately rode off towards the mountain peak and soon came back with some snow. The ruler asked loudly so that all the other servants may hear – "How did you know I wanted some snow?"

The reply came – **"Because you stared at it longingly, and your look expressed your desire to possess some."**

The ruler smiled and told the others – "**I gave him a special place, because for every person there is a chosen occupation, and his occupation is observing my glances and watching my states of being attentively.**"

Can you make your customers feel the same way? It is definitely possible.

But only when you focus and pay complete attention to your customer's words, expressions and body language, and not be eager to demonstrate what you can provide at the expense of learning what the customer wants.

When you are with your customer, your approach should be – **Nothing else matters.**

It has been scientifically proven that multi-tasking, or attempting to do more than one activity at a time, dilutes the quality of one's output. So, when you are supposed to be listening with all your senses, mind and soul, no other thought must interfere with this vital flow of inputs coming from the most important person in the entire business world – **Your Customer.**

When you listen with total concentration, it is possible for you to provide your customer with customised service through personalised attention, providing beyond what your competitors or other salespersons may attempt to provide.

It may also sometimes happen that the prospect you are dealing with is unable to express his thoughts and requirements clearly. It is possible that this may happen quite often. This is when you need to concentrate and listen even more actively than you usually do.

As someone said – **When the speaker is weak, the listener must be exceptionally strong.**

When you think beyond your own products and services, you are thinking more in terms of your customer's convenience. This puts you in a favourable position in the mind of the customer.

As an example, the restaurant **'Pali Presidency'**, is one among many restaurants in the suburb of Bandra in Mumbai. Each of these restaurants provide their customers with a takeaway menu, by which they can order packed meals from these restaurants to their residences. A huge chunk of the business of these restaurants comes from such takeaway orders.

While the takeaway menus of other restaurants have the name of their restaurant and other related details printed in bold on the front page, the takeaway menu of the 'Pali Presidency' does something positively different.

'Pali Presidency' has a listing on the front page in bold print, of the **contact details of all Emergency Services in the locality,** assuming that most of its takeaway orders would come from customers in the nearby vicinity.

No other restaurant in the locality has thought of this customised extra. The 'Pali Presidency' has taken time and listened to an unspoken need that its customers have.

Can you guess whose takeaway menu out of all other restaurant menus is always kept at the top of the pile by the customer at his residence?

The Brains Trust Pearl:
True listening happens when body, heart, mind and soul come together.

8

If you meet all your commitments,
once you've given your valuable word

In the minds of your customers,
you'll always be first, second and third

Boasts are harder to honour than promises.

- Unknown

It is a very tempting proposition to over-promise and thoroughly impress the customer during your presentation. But if all that you have promised and committed to your customer during your presentation and sales pitch is **NOT** delivered once you have secured the order, you have lost a customer and all the referrals you could have got through him for life.

But if you **DO** meet your commitments once you've given your valuable word, and the customer as a result develops total trust and implicit faith in all that you say, you have permanently eliminated all competitors from the minds of your customers.

Thereafter, in the minds of your customers, there will be no room for ANY salesperson other than yourself in your product or service category.

In the minds of your customers, you will truly be first, second as well as third.

So it is important to be mature during your presentation, and not overenthusiastic or on the edge of your seat. It is important to remain rational in your approach (so that you do not make rash commitments you could never hope to meet.) But bear in mind that your objective is to stimulate rational as well as emotional interest in your prospect.

And if you **DO** erroneously over-promise, you should then do your utmost to keep the promise you have made. It is not just a promise. It is your reputation at stake.

It may mean making things a little inconvenient for you in the short run. It may mean a little more effort, a little running around, a little extra expense.

But believe us – **IT IS WELL WORTH IT.**

Anyone can be an ACE :
Attitude + Commitment + Excellence.

- Robert Inman

Both us authors are in love with the **Crown Plaza Hotel** located near **Venice** in **Italy,** although neither of us has been to Italy in our living days.

The love affair exists because of an incident which occurred involving this particular hotel in August 2009.

This Five Star Hotel, which **normally charges** a room rate of between **Euro Ninety and Euro One Hundred and Fifty ($130 - $215), per night, mistakenly offered** the ultimate, dream, low-cost vacation – **A Five Star weekend in this romantic city of Venice for ONE EURO CENT PER NIGHT.**

This unbelievably low rate was posted on the hotel's website, and within the few hours that the erroneous rate was displayed on the website, **Monica Smith,** (the hotel's Media Relations Manager in the United States), said that the hotel received reservations from 228 guests, who made reservations for the equivalent of 1,400 room nights at **ONE EURO CENT.**

At first, the hotel management thought that the offer was posted by a hacker, but it was later found that it was the **result of genuine human error at the Atlanta, Georgia, offices of Intercontinental Hotels Group, the hotel's mother company.**

The offer was actually meant to be for a two night stay at half price. The erroneous one cent rate was up on the website only for one Sunday night, but that was long enough for the 228 travelers to book dates at one cent right till October 2010.

"The hotel stands to lose Euro Ninety Thousand ($129,000)", said **Fulvio Danesin,** the Sales Manager of the Crown Plaza.

"But", said the Media Relations Manager, **"although a pricing error, Intercontinental Hotels is COMMITTED to honouring the one cent rate for guests who have a valid confirmation."**

This brilliantly customer oriented gesture received world wide publicity (that's how we got to hear of it), and generated unbelievable positive word-of-mouth publicity for the hotel group. Sounds unbelievable. But every word is true.

Honour your commitments with integrity.

- Les Brown

Contrast the approach of the Crown Plaza Hotel with that of a chain of parlours of a so-called 'premium' ice-cream brand in Mumbai. This parlour advertised at the beginning of a particular month in the local newspapers that a particular flavour of ice-cream would be sold for Rupees Ten, instead of the regular price of around Rupees Seventy. The advertisement clearly mentioned that the offer was valid for the **first WEEK of the month** at all its outlets.

For customers who visited the outlets on the **first DAY of the month**, the commitment was honoured. But all other customers (us included), who went to the outlets from the 2nd to the 7th of that month, (the first week), in response to the advertisement, were blatantly told – **"Sorry, it was a misprint by our advertising agency. We intended to keep the offer only for the first day of the month. Not the entire first week. If you want the ice-cream, you can now have it at full price."**

This negative response was sufficient to turn many customers off this brand for a lifetime.

There's a difference between interest and commitment.
When you're interested in doing something, you do it only
when circumstances permit. When you're committed to
something, you accept no excuses, only results.

- Unknown

44

Any customer, who has been given **one single reason** to doubt the word of an organisation or a salesperson, will start to doubt the integrity of **EVERY** statement and claim that the brand or salesperson makes henceforth. Such an organisation or salesperson would **never be** the preferred choice for that product or service category for that customer.

It is said:

A burnt child fears the fire.

It is also said, and rightly so:

If wealth is lost, nothing is lost.
If health is lost, something is lost.
If reputation is lost, everything is lost.

And to sum it up, the following provides great food for thought.

Commitment unlocks the door of imagination, allows vision, and gives us the 'right stuff' to turn our dreams into reality.

- James Womack

The Brains Trust Pearl:
Do your homework thoroughly before you make any commitment to a customer. But once you commit, your job is to deliver. Regardless.

9

Punctuality is impressive,
punctuality is the key

This simple rule is oft forgotten,
but it leads from 'You' and 'I' to 'We'

In the process of selling, the act of punctuality in all its aspects creates a bond; a feeling of oneness, a 'WE' feeling.

Punctuality is the first sign of respect and dependability.
- Cyrus M Gonda, Dr. Kalim Khan

Being punctual reflects a healthy and positive attitude.

If you as a salesperson are not bothered about your customer's time, (which is his most valuable and scarce resource), you are giving a clear message that you are not bothered about the customer either.

An ancient Indian proverb rightly says - **Punctuality is the politeness of princes.**

And surely you would want to be a **prince among salespersons?**

Punctuality can be displayed and demonstrated in various situations. It is not only about being on time, but it is also about timely fulfillment of commitments, and timely response to given situations.

- Reaching the place of appointment not just on time but slightly before time
- Being prompt in responding to customer queries
- Providing delivery as per committed schedule

The above are just three examples of situations where the customer expects you to be punctual.

When you have a meeting scheduled, ensure that you reach the meeting place a little prior to the meeting time. This allows time for you to freshen up and look and feel your best. You should not reach in a rush and in a hurry. If you reach before time, you will then be calm and composed and at your intellectual and physical best when you interact with the prospective customer. You will then also be in a better position to explain the credibility of your brand to your client in the best manner possible.

When **Sir Isaac Newton** coined the word 'inertia', little did he realise that it would hold true more for human sciences than for physical sciences.

We all as human beings tend to fall in comfort zones and it is practically impossible for us to come out of habits that keep us cosy.

Salespersons need to identify their personal habits of inertia and rectify them. Some very strong habits indicating inertia are; **lethargy, procrastination** and **late-coming.**

As academicians, we have realised that punctuality as a trait emanates from student days, and those who are punctual as students are punctual for a life-time. Such individuals inevitably make conscious attempts to ensure punctuality at all costs at all times on all occasions.

A very strong message for all budding salespersons comes from us in the form of a **formula** –

Customer Respect = Punctuality X Responsiveness

We would like to emphasise that the habit of punctuality is not simply about being punctual for client meetings. We have seen umpteen salespersons reaching on time for initial client meetings, creating a good impression, and then proceeding to destroy it by not responding in time to client requests for information or for follow-ups.

A customer's time is of extreme importance to him and all sales and service providers need to realise this.

An excellent example of this fanatical attention to customer time comes from the world famous brand – **Walt Disney World.** At the multiple rides in the Walt Disney World, long queues of patrons wishing to enjoy these rides are always eagerly formed. The management at Walt Disney World carefully monitors each queue, constantly calculating how much time a person at a particular position in the queue would take before he would get on the ride.

The persons in the queue are regularly informed about the waiting time they have left based on their location in the queue, and if the calculation shows they would take fifteen minutes, they are told that it would take twenty minutes, as **the management has a fantastic policy of under-promising and over-delivering. This policy is a constant source of customer delight.**

It is akin to a salesperson telling a customer that delivery would take a maximum of five days, fully knowing even at the time that he makes that commitment, that he would be ensuring delivery in four days, or even in three.

The following is a fantastic example of punctuality in all its forms, that salespersons could profitably emulate.

A friend of ours who runs a retail outlet was in the process of identifying a service provider for developing his software and website. Since he is a meticulous person, he naturally had a list of queries regarding the various activities he could perform with the software, such as inventory control, billing, storing customer requests, and the like.

He sent email queries to four software providers cum website developers whom he identified from the Yellow Pages.

One of these so-called 'service providers' never bothered to respond to his query at all.

Two of them were delayed, shabby and vague in their response.

The fourth was brilliant. He responded immediately and told our friend that he would get back with specific answers to all his queries **within two days.** (Our friend had listed forty one queries pertaining to his unique requirements of the software and website in his initial query.)

The following is what that brilliant fourth service provider, (a Super Salesperson), did:

- The fourth service provider had said he would get back within two days, but he got back to our friend within only a day
- He responded to each of the forty one queries, making a separate document highlighting each of our friend's queries in large font, and putting down his response to that query below it in small font
- He clearly explained whether each individual query could be solved by using his software, and to what extent the software would be useful for our friend's purpose
- He also added queries of his own with regard to the software and website requirements of the retail outlet which our friend had not even considered initially
- His language was clear, polite and accurate
- His response was more than prompt

Although the fees this salesperson quoted were slightly on the higher side, **NO PRIZES FOR GUESSING WHO WAS AWARDED THE CONTRACT.**

How much does a punctual and comprehensive response such as this cost the salesperson?

A little time and a little effort.

What are the benefits for the salesperson?

A guaranteed sale at a premium price point, as well as securing a customer for life.

The only thing that surprises us is the fact that more salespersons are not emulating this highly profitable example.

So the key to sales success lies in finding out exactly what your client needs. And then proceeding to remove the bridge between you and him by doing it promptly.

A handyman once put an advertisement in the newspaper advertising his services.

The advertisement went as follows:

'I can fix anything your husband can. And I'll fix it NOW.'

The Brains Trust Pearl:
You have no right to ever keep your customer waiting

10

Love what you're selling, that's important;
that is something you should do

Only if you love your product,
will your prospect love it too

It has been rightly said – **Select a job that you love, and you will never have to work a day in your life.**

This love should also extend to your product, your profession, your industry and your customer.

When we as human beings interact with one another, it has been scientifically proven that we sub-consciously send out signals in the form of vibrations, which the opposite party picks up. These vibrations, both negative as well as positive, are stronger than we could ever imagine them to be. They create a substantial impact about us in the mind, and ultimately in the decision making process, of the person we are dealing with.

A salesperson's genuine love for the product or service he represents generates strong, positive vibrations, which the other party responds to positively.

This is the main reason why experienced interviewers prefer to recruit and select salespersons that appear to be truly passionate about the product or service they are being selected to sell.

Think enthusiastically about everything, but especially about your job. If you do, you'll put a touch of glory in your life. If you love your job with enthusiasm, you'll shake it to pieces. You'll love it into greatness.

\- Norman Vincent Peale

It is not always possible for us to enter the industry which is our first choice in terms of area of interest. That is a fact of life. But it is **ALWAYS** possible for us to make the best of the situation we are in.

And in every product or service, there is always some element we can learn to love. Identify that element and proceed with your sales presentation with genuine passion. Your presentation will be a breeze.

Even in the area of Public Speaking, we can clearly see the difference in a person when he is speaking on just any topic, compared with the manner in which the same person speaks when he is speaking on a topic he is passionate about.

When he speaks on something which he truly believes in, you will hear fire in his voice and see fire in his eyes.

He will convert his audience to endorse and support his point of view on the strength of the passion he generates.

Similarly, when you truly love the product or service you are selling, your genuine passion and love for the product or service will come through loud and clear during your sales presentation, and will positively impact your prospect as well.

If you can't have what you love, you should learn to love what you have.

Harry Winston, a famous New York diamond dealer, once called a wealthy diamond collector about a new diamond that he might want to add to his collection. The collector flew to New York, and one of Winston's salesmen showed him the diamond. The salesman explained in detail about all the technical features of the diamond. The customer politely said – "It's a beautiful diamond, but not exactly what I want."

When the customer was about to leave the store, Winston himself decided to display the diamond to him. When Winston finished explaining the qualities of the diamond, the man immediately bought it. Winston asked the reason why he had changed his mind, although it was the same diamond which had been displayed during both the presentations.

The answer the customer gave was – "Your salesman **KNOWS** diamonds, but you **LOVE** them."

Before salesmen sell anything to anyone, they must first sell it to themselves.

- Unknown

John Sculley, who was named **Silicon Valley's top paid executive in 1987 as CEO of Apple,** had previously worked with the Pepsi Corporation.

In his autobiography, Sculley explains the reason for his **shift from Pepsi to Apple.**

He says he was financially and professionally secure with Pepsi, but Steve Jobs, the then CEO of Apple, approached Sculley and asked him – "Do you want to spend the rest of your life selling sugared water, or do you want a chance to change the world?"

The rest is marketing history.

That wise man, **Aristotle,** said – 'Pleasure in the job puts perfection in the work.'

In no way are we suggesting that every person in the profession of selling aerated colas should shift over to selling personal computers. The point is, Sculley thought over his options, and decided **HIS** passion and interest lay with the products Apple was innovating. He attributes his career as a super successful salesperson to making the choice of following his heart.

As we said before – **Only if you love your product, will your prospect love it too.**

Even an arranged marriage needs to flower into love if it is to survive, thrive and blossom.

– Cyrus M Gonda, Dr. Kalim Khan

The Brains Trust Pearl:
Love your job. Love your brand. You will receive love and financial rewards in return.

11

Learn all you can about your profession,
you've chosen it to make your life

Acquire all the knowledge that's possible,
your career will then be free of strife

Menus do not exist only in restaurants.

Every organisation in every industry has its own unique menu, which consists of the entire range of products and services that it offers its customers.

In the same way that a good service person in a restaurant ought to be aware of, and familiarise himself with:

- Every possible aspect of every item on his restaurant menu
- The subtle differences in taste between two dishes
- The ingredients they contain
- The style of preparation

Similarly every Super Salesperson should familiarise himself with every article in his sales stable.

It is a safe bet that twenty percent of the product or service offerings in your sales portfolio will be asked for by eighty percent of your prospects and customers eighty percent of the time.

It makes sense for you to first be thoroughly familiar with every aspect of these twenty percent of your offerings. These will constitute the bread and butter of your sales volumes.

Once you attain thorough knowledge of these, your next immediate task should be to make yourself familiar with the intricate aspects of the balance eighty percent of the offerings on your menu, which will constitute the jam and cheese of your sales.

Don't just satisfy yourself with acquiring information about the basic features and functioning of your offerings. Master them in totality.

There is **ALWAYS** more to learn.

Be prepared for the tricky customer queries, the loopholes with regards to product functioning, what product and service customisation is possible, how much time such customisation would take, and so on.

In short, become a walking, talking encyclopedia as far as your range of products and services are concerned.

It may sound difficult to do, but all it really requires is good, old fashioned effort. Regular, relevant reading is absolutely essential.

This is possible for salespersons to do, irrespective of the industry in which they operate. And it is absolutely necessary if you want to make it big in this highly competitive world of selling.

Learning is not compulsory......neither is survival.

\- W Edwards Deming

Reflect on the joy you feel when you hire a taxi and tell the driver your destination, and the taxi driver immediately understands where you wish to reach, and takes you there by the shortest possible route, which has the least possible traffic. These are the taxi drivers who get the largest tips. (In fact, the origin of the word **TIPS** is the term – **To Insure Prompt Service.**)

It is only possible for you to provide prompt and efficient service when you have attained mastery of product and service knowledge. **The huge tips you then receive as a salesperson will be in the form of increased sales volumes and profitable referrals from delighted customers.**

Exceptional and outstanding taxi drivers take a healthy interest in their job:

- They understand that the same destination is known by different names by different sets of people and learn all these names
- They keep in mind the landmarks that customers use as terms to define their destination
- They acquire knowledge of multiple routes leading to the same destination
- They are also able to identify the time of day when each of these routes would have the least traffic

Similarly, a Super Salesperson will familiarise himself as soon as possible with the finer aspects of every article he is selling. His goal should be to ensure that for any and every query, (however out of the way), that any potential customer may put forward regarding any aspect of the product or service being offered by him for sale; a clear, crisp and correct answer should be ready on the mind and on the lips of the Super Salesperson.

Test yourself for improvement in this vital area on a regular basis.

Constantly and consciously make efforts and **ask yourself at the end of every week - 'What is that SOMETHING new which I learnt this week about my products or services?'**

Note these points down in a book, and in six months time, you will be amazingly pleased with the amount of relevant information you have gathered. Once this information is yours, you will be able to make a prospect understand **WHY** he should prefer **YOUR** brand of product or service, as well as why he should buy it from **YOU**. (So that he can get the benefit of your superior knowledge and expertise, of course.) Once you are thorough with these aspects, watch your sales zoom.

Learning is not attained by chance, it must be sought for with ardor and attended to with diligence.

- Abigail Adams

Huge volumes of sales are lost each day because the prospect is not convinced and satisfied with the salesperson's answers and responses to his queries.

Many unprepared salespersons give vague and ambiguous responses, or brush aside valid customer queries, simply because the salesperson himself lacks clarity and proper knowledge.

Develop a passionate hunger for learning.
Your meals can wait. Learning cannot.

— Cyrus M Gonda, Dr. Kalim Khan

The following lovely true story which appears in the **autobiography of P T Barnum**, (Struggles and Triumphs), gives you a good idea as to the extreme level of learning that certain individuals aspire to acquire about the products and services that it is their job to deal with.

Cuvier, a French naturalist, thoroughly knew his business. So proficient was he in the study of natural history, that you might bring him a bone or even the part of a bone of an animal which he had never seen, and by reasoning from analogy, he would be able to mentally draw an accurate and complete picture of the creature from which the bone had been taken.

On one occasion, his students attempted to deceive him. They rolled one of themselves in a cow skin and put him under the professor's table as a new specimen. When Cuvier came into the room, some of the students asked him what animal it was. Suddenly, the 'animal' rose up and said – "I am the devil and I am going to eat you."

It was but natural that Cuvier, given his extreme passion and knowledge about his subject, should desire to classify this creature, and observing and examining it immediately and intently, said – **"Divided hoof, graminovorous, it cannot eat me."**

Even in a moment of extreme stress and apparent danger, the great and knowledgeable Cuvier spontaneously observed and reasoned that an animal with a split hoof (which the cow skin had), must live upon grass and grain, or other kind of vegetation (graminovorous by nature), and hence would not be inclined to eat flesh, dead or alive, so he considered himself perfectly safe.

The possession of perfect knowledge of your business is an absolute necessity in order to ensure success.

The wisest mind has something yet to learn.

- George Santayana

Motivate yourself to reach the level of learning that Cuvier reached through his hard work and dedication, so much so that even if you're woken from your sleep, the specific attributes of your products and services are at your fingertips.

The more you know about your products and services, the better and more clearly you will be able to explain these to your prospect, the lesser will be the grievances and complaints that he as a customer will burden you with later.

- Cyrus M Gonda, Dr. Kalim Khan

The Brains Trust Pearl:
Satisfy your hunger for learning. In an indirect way, this will fill your stomach.

12

But indifference is a killer,
indifference you must shun

In a salesperson's mind this should be foremost,
that away from indifference you must run

A Super Salesperson is always on the lookout for and is hungry for sensing a business opportunity. He noses out customer needs like a bloodhound, and does his utmost to service those needs.

But strange to relate, it is amazing to see many platinum opportunities for business being callously lost by leading brands today. Business which is literally falling into the lap is being pushed away by indifferent salespersons and even store managers.

They say that death kills you, but death doesn't kill you. Boredom and indifference kill you.

- Iggy Pop

A simple recent example we witnessed, (one of many such examples), says it all.

We were at a leading outlet of a premier shoe chain and asked to see some formal shoes. Whichever design we liked was not available in our size with the store.

Fair enough.

But what followed was unacceptable. None of the store attendants could tell us when the design of our choice would be available in our size, (if at all.) We asked them to check with their head office or factory and get the information. Their reply was - **"That won't be of any help. Nobody anywhere knows anything. If the sizes come, they come."**

Neither did they have any catalogue which could be referred to for information about new designs, or when they would arrive.

They couldn't tell us whether a design that was currently in stock would be repeated or discontinued from next month onwards.

In short, they were as clueless about almost every aspect of their own brand as we as outsiders were.

While we were being attended to (or **un-attended** to, if there is such a word), we heard a commotion at the cash counter and turned to have a look.

A polished lady was yelling in well accented tones at the person at the cash counter. **"You guys must be crazy"**, she was saying in a raised voice, over and over again. Then she saw us looking at her enquiringly and came over to us to explain her outburst and to vent her frustration. **"I'm here to purchase a gift coupon for their shoes which these guys proudly advertise that they sell. I need it to present for someone's birthday tomorrow. I thought it would make a nice gift. So I came here as this is a premium outlet of their shoe chain. But when I asked for a Rupees Two Thousand worth gift coupon, this guy at the cash counter tells me to email at the address of some guy in their head office where their marketing department is located and procure the coupons from him. I am giving them business and they expect me to do all the work and running around. These guys are crazy,"** she repeated as she stormed out of the shoe store.

We could empathise with her.

We walked out as well.

Positive thinking coupled with positive actions puts you past the victory line in sales as well as in life.

- Cyrus M Gonda, Dr. Kalim Khan

Another recent incident which comes to our mind goes as follows.

We saw a neat HP laptop backpack model which a friend of ours had picked up from a computer store at Lamington Road in South Mumbai. Since Lamington Road is a bit out of the way for us, we visited a dedicated HP World outlet in our vicinity. It was a fairly large sized store, well furnished, situated in a premium suburban location and dedicated only to HP products. The rent being paid for that outlet would have been nothing short of Rupees Two

Lakhs a month. We reached the outlet on a weekday at around 2 p.m. There was no other customer in the store at that time. The owner/manager was seated at the cash counter, face dipped into his accounts register, in which he was engrossed. We stood directly in front of him for at least twenty seconds before he realised that some customers had entered his store. We politely asked to see the backpacks for laptops.

Without taking the effort to even greet us, he shouted across the store to the only helper/assistant present, asking him to show us the backpacks they had in stock, and promptly dug his nose back into his accounts register. The helper/assistant showed us two models of backpacks, none of which remotely resembled the smart HP backpack our friend had purchased. We returned to the owner/manager at the counter, disturbed him from his engrossing task, and asked him if he had any other models in stock. **"Only these two"**, was what he said, before going back to his accounts register.

We patiently told him about the HP backpack our friend had purchased just the week before and even gave him the model number of the backpack, which we had taken down from our friend. We asked him if he could get it for us. His answer was a brief – **"No"**, which was said in an irritated tone and without looking up. We asked him where it could be available. **"Try the HP helpline"**, he said.

That's when we walked out. The next day we went to Lamington Road, where almost every computer store (even though they were not dedicated HP outlets), stocked the backpack we were looking for. We bought the backpacks from the store where we got the best bargain. (Rupees One Thousand Six Hundred each.)

Indifference and neglect often do much more damage than outright dislike.

- J K Rowling

There are multiple similar examples we could quote where leading brands are involved. Many of these occur in premium outlets of premium brands, where the rents must be astronomical.

It is almost as if some people have set up shop to pass their time.

Unfortunately such incidents have become all too common today, and many of us can relate to and identify with them.

> *It is almost as if some people in business today are saying,*
> *"Thanks a lot. We can do without your business."*
>
> - Cyrus M Gonda, Dr. Kalim Khan

The lesson for Super Brands and Super Salespersons is that they need to be **HUNGRY** for business.

Never ever let a lethargic and indifferent attitude lose you a single customer.

A friend of ours, who runs a retail store, wanted to buy a printer for his computer. Someone recommended a vendor who would give him a printer at the best price. Our friend called him up, specified the model of printer he required, and the vendor committed that he would have it delivered the next day. Our friend patiently waited for two days but no printer came. On the third day, when our friend enquired when it would be delivered, as his printing work was getting delayed, the vendor told him bluntly without apologising – "I didn't have a delivery person available." Since our friend was himself going near the locality of this shop that evening, he decided to pick up the printer on his way.

He asked the vendor if he could just SMS him the address of his store and he would pick it up himself, sparing the vendor the effort and cost of having it delivered. The vendor replied – **"I'm busy. My address is too long for me to type out and SMS. I'll dictate it, you write it down."**

Our friend hung up and bought the printer at a slightly higher price from elsewhere.

He rightly felt that if this was the attitude of the vendor **BEFORE** he made the sale, what would the pathetic and lethargic after-sales-service be like, if any were required. The vendor lost a Rupees Eight Thousand sale and many other sales which he could have got through our friend through positive word-of-mouth referrals.

The amazing fact is, all these incidents we have narrated have occurred during the peak of recession, when organisations are crying for lack of business.

> *Love me or hate me, but spare me your indifference.*
>
> - Libbie Fudim

A positive example follows, well worth learning from and emulating.

As a Management Institute, we wanted to engage the services of a service provider for Bulk SMSes which would be used for sending common messages to individuals on our institute database, informing them about various institute events and happenings. We got a list of such providers in our locality from the internet, and got in the act of contacting some of them to identify a suitable vendor for the same.

As we were not very comfortable with this technology, we requested the people who advertised this service if they could personally come over and demonstrate and explain how the service worked.

The varied responses from each of them taught us how business could be lost due to sheer indifference and an attitude of 'No care'.

A common response was – "We are very busy and find it difficult to leave office. You could go through our website. It is self explanatory. You could write us a mail in case of any queries. And once you pay and book the order online, the services shall be initiated."

The firm which won our order had a different response. The fact is that even they did not personally turn up to meet us. **What they did was something even better:**

- The person we called understood our requirements, then requested if he could get back in a couple of minutes
- In the meanwhile he seemingly checked our website and credentials to learn a little about us. He soon called us back, and said he wouldn't mind coming over personally, but if we could call a technical person from our computer laboratory at our side and open his website, he would hold on
- His confident voice, tone and language made us do exactly what he wanted us to do
- He didn't make us call and keep us on hold, he himself called and kept himself on hold. Bravo!
- We got our lab person by our side and opened his website
- Then he said he would navigate us through his entire website and thus patiently explained how the entire process and service worked
- After we had understood, and were satisfied, we negotiated a rate for a hundred thousand bulk SMSes. (All this during that same telephone call.)
- Once we were satisfied with the rate he quoted, he asked us how we would like to make the payment
- Since we said we were not comfortable with the method of paying online, and asked if we could pay by cheque, he said that was perfectly fine
- He told us he would initiate the activity immediately for us to use and that we could deposit the cheque in a bank account, the details of which he provided us
- **Last but not the least, he asked us if we would still want him to come down in person. You can guess that there was no need for us to trouble him**

Indifference is the strongest force in the universe. It makes everything it touches meaningless. Love and hate don't stand a chance against it.

- Joan Vinge

The Brains Trust Pearl:
The disease of indifference marks the demise of a sales career.

13

Do that extra, little extra,
always go the extra mile

In any business this is possible,
it helps your business run in style

Our favourite business quotation of all time comes from a gentleman named **Roger Staubach**. It goes as follows.

"There are no traffic jams along the extra mile."

It is self explanatory.

As customers, we would all love to be served and attended to by the salesperson or service provider who takes that one extra step to make life more convenient for us.

But it is surprising that when we are on the other side of the table, (that is, when we play the role of salespersons in our business), many of us salespersons tend to cut corners and take short cuts.

If you are willing to go the extra mile, there is a world of customers waiting at the end of that mile, eager to be served.

- Cyrus M Gonda, Dr. Kalim Khan

Customers yearn to identify salespersons that go out of their way for them, and will stick to these salespersons like glue.

You can start right where you stand and apply the habit of going the extra mile by rendering more service and better service than you are now being paid for.

- Napoleon Hill

The following is an example of the multiple gains that going out of your way for a customer can bring for you as a salesperson.

We were once conducting a four day workshop on Customer Service, which was scheduled to be conducted over two simultaneous weekends.

The profile of the participants in this workshop ranged from across the spectrum of working life. Some were employed with organisations in different industries, others had their own businesses in different fields. One of these participants was a young gentleman named Yusuf Bharmal, who owns and manages a pharmaceutical store in South Mumbai.

During the first two days of the workshop, we explained the importance of going the extra mile for the customer, and the advantages it would bring to the salesperson. Then there was a break for a week, before the workshop resumed on the next weekend. When we resumed, we asked the participants if they had managed to implement any of the inputs we had discussed on the first two days. Immediately, Yusuf raised his hand excitedly and narrated the following incident.

He told us that he ran a pharmaceutical store in a locality where many other pharmaceutical stores were also located. During this last week, a patient carrying a doctor's prescription approached him. There were three medicines listed by the doctor on that prescription, of which the patient had already purchased two from another store. The third not being in stock in other stores, the patient approached Yusuf with the hope that it would be available here. Yusuf didn't have it in stock either. Here comes the critical part of the tale.

Yusuf continued, saying that a week ago, he would have behaved like all the other store keepers had, telling the patient that it was not in stock, that he had a couple of medicines which could possibly serve as alternatives, and leave it to the patient's judgment whether he purchased any of the alternatives or not.

But after listening to our talk on going the extra mile, he decided to put the philosophy into practice, now that he had an opportunity to do so:

- Yusuf took the prescription from the patient, and identified two alternatives to the medicine which was not in stock
- He then called up the doctor at his clinic, taking the number of the clinic from the doctor's prescription
- He identified himself as a pharmaceutical store owner to whom the doctor's patient had arrived
- He explained that one of the medicines prescribed was not in stock
- He also mentioned the two alternatives that he as a pharmacist felt were suitable, and asked the doctor as to which of the two would be more suitable for his patient
- He also made the patient personally speak with the doctor

The patient purchased the alternative that the doctor recommended, thanked Yusuf profusely, and went off.

The story doesn't end there.

Within fifteen minutes, the patient returned to Yusuf.

He said that he had gone to the store from which he had purchased the first two medicines and had returned them and had taken a refund.

He told Yusuf that he wanted to purchase those two medicines also from Yusuf's store.

His words were – **"You have taken the extra effort for me that other store keepers did not bother to do. I don't see why I should buy anything from them. You deserve to get all my business, not only now, but also in the future. And be sure I will tell all possible people I know in the locality to come to you for any pharmaceutical related needs."**

Come to think of it, in most businesses, there is no way in which salespersons and service providers can differentiate themselves from their competitors, apart from going the extra mile to provide that little extra service.

And customers notice and appreciate this extra effort, and reciprocate.

Do more than is required. What is the distance between someone who achieves their goals consistently and those who spend their lives and careers merely following?
The extra mile.

- Gary Ryan Blair

The Brains Trust Pearl:
Willingly go the extra mile for your customer. Your reward waits at its end, like the pot of gold waits at the end of the rainbow.

14

It is said 'Knowledge is Power',
this is also true for sales

Collect data, analyse data,
this road to selling never fails

We previously mentioned about the knowledge that a salesperson must acquire about his profession. That knowledge is a must. But mere knowledge of the profession, though vital, is by itself not sufficient. For a salesperson to be a success, knowledge of other, related areas is also crucial for success. The higher the interest level that you as a salesperson develop in doing your job well, the more will be the data and information you will seek a continuous basis. That is what will elevate you to the category of an **EXPERT**.

For a salesperson, various categories of knowledge are essential to achieve success:

- Technical knowledge
- Market knowledge
- Commercial knowledge
- Knowledge about the customer

Sir Don Bradman, the greatest batsman of all time with a batting average of 99.94 in test cricket, knew the power of acquiring thorough knowledge in **ALL** areas related to one's chosen profession.

In his superb book, 'The Art of Cricket', the great Bradman mentions that cricket captains should not only be good players on the field, they must also be fully aware of the laws of the game of cricket. Not many are aware that **Bradman himself studied for and passed the umpire's exam and was a qualified umpire. He also opined that a cricket captain should be an avid reader on the evolution, history, the traditions and the culture of the game.**

All knowledge comes from information.

And accurate information comes from proper data. (Information is nothing but processed data.)

And just as in computer parlance, a term known as **GIGO (Garbage In – Garbage Out)**, is important, it holds equally true for the sales profession.

The quality of the data that you constantly forage for matters tremendously.

Do you merely know what other salespersons also know, or have you stretched out your hands and your mind in various directions, to gather information which other salespersons may have overlooked?

Knowledge about the customer is also critical. The customer would want you to be as well informed about him as possible. It is similar to a job interview, where all other things being equal, the job applicant who has taken effort to know more about the organisation where he is applying, is most likely to get the job.

There are multiple sources from which you can generate information about the customer and his organisation. Never stop learning, even till the last minute.

For example, once you make it a practice to reach a little before time for a client meet, you can invest time at the **reception area** of the client organisation.

Here, you can read his in-house journal and other company literature, observe the awards, certificates and trophies which the client organisation has won, and which are normally displayed in the reception area. These will provide you with a lot of useful information about the client organisation, as well as give you content for conversing with the client.

So as you see, learning never stops. Acquire a hunger and thirst for knowledge which burns your insides till it is satiated.

The more the importance given by the salesperson to the gathering of relevant data, and to the processing of that data into useful information, the better will be the quality of interaction with and the service provided to the prospective customer.

In many organisations, expensive knowledge providing software has been installed, but the staff there has not been sufficiently trained in what data to collect and what data to generate. The entire investment on software and hardware in such scenarios is nothing but a sheer waste.

A recent example of how lack of market knowledge cost a salesperson a customer follows. And such examples are frequently being experienced by many of us.

One of us authors recently received a telemarketing call from a salesperson representing a leading private sector health-insurance organisation. Since the author was genuinely considering the purchase of a health-insurance policy at that moment of time, this seemed like a good opportunity to do so.

The author naturally asked the salesperson – "Can you tell me how your policy differs from the policies of other health-insurance firms and how the plan you are offering is superior to the plans offered by other insurance firms?"

It was a very valid question which almost any prospect would wish to clarify before purchasing health-insurance.

But the response from the salesperson was an indignant – **"Sir, I can at the most tell you details about the insurance policies and plans that OUR company offers. How can I be expected to know details about the competitor's policies?"**

Although we are not aware of the number of sales opportunities that the company might have lost due to such a pathetic response, but we are sure, that the volume must be huge.

Unless you possess market knowledge and are aware of the attributes of the products of your competitors, how can you identify the USPs of your own product or service? (USPs are ultimately nothing but the competitive advantages that your products and services enjoy over those of your competitors.)

We are not intending that you speak negatively about your competitor or his products. We are against such practices. But when a customer specifically asks you how your product or service compares with, or how it differentiates from similar products and services available in the market, it is your duty as a salesperson to be aware of the market scenario and educate your prospect about the same.

Contrast the above example of half-baked knowledge with a brilliantly positive example of **Mr. Manoj** of **Manoj Pen Mart**. It is a small store located in South Mumbai, run by Manoj, his brother Kishore, and their father.

For all purchases related to any kind of writing instruments, we would whole-heartedly recommend anyone to visit Manoj.

He knows the intricacies of every aspect of every pen and pencil that passes through his hands, and what is more, he takes time to patiently explain these intricacies to each customer. He has a story to relate about every model of pen he stocks.

We were once admiring a fine, shining pen and were in two minds whether to purchase it or not. We asked him which metal it was made of:

- Manoj immediately explained that high end pens could be made from any one of five similar looking metals – Platinum, Rhodium, Palladium, Silver or Steel. He explained their order of ranking in terms of strength and durability, and also the unique qualities of each of them

- He then displayed a high end pen with a body partially made of wood. He explained that the company which made this pen had its own timber farms at a particular location in Europe. The trees from these farms alone were used to make the wooden part of these pens, as the company followed strict quality control of raw material used

- He also explained to us in detail the difference between a Limited Edition pen and a Special Edition pen

- And in the course of the discussion he has enlightened us with the history of the fountain-pen and the ball-pen and told us in which year the first of them was ever manufactured and sold and by which company

And all this is just a fraction of the informative and entertaining knowledge that we have learnt about writing instruments through Manoj. He is more than a walking encyclopedia as far as his field goes. As he knows the intricate details of every product he demonstrates, it gives a great feeling of confidence to his customers.

If the salesperson himself lacks detailed knowledge about his products and services, how could he be expected to guide the prospect towards a sensible and suitable choice and to a correct purchase decision?

- Cyrus M Gonda, Dr. Kalim Khan

We asked Manoj why he didn't enter into business in a related field such as wrist watches, (pens and watches both being articles of dress accessory.)

His reply was impressive. "Since I don't have thorough domain knowledge of wrist watches, I would not wish to enter that field until I first acquire the requisite knowledge."

His deep knowledge of pens translates into huge sales and loyal customers galore.

Even in plush malls, we have observed salespersons manning the counters of reputed pen brands, who in most cases would be at a loss to provide a small percentage of the information to their customers that Manoj is well known for.

If money is your hope for independence you will never have it. The only real security that a man will have in this world is a reserve of knowledge, experience and ability.

- Henry Ford

We had recently visited an electronics store to understand and compare the features of laptops and notebooks of different brands. The store stocked multiple brands of laptops, each brand having an assigned salesperson to demonstrate its products. At almost every counter, we were highly disgruntled and irritated with the lethargy, incompetence and lack of information and knowledge displayed by the salespersons there. It seemed they were just not interested in business, and if at all a sale had to happen, then the only possibility was that it would happen by default, with a customer coming in pre-decided to purchase a particular model of a particular brand.

But the silver lining on this dark cloud appeared when we reached the counter where notebooks of the brand '**Apple**' were displayed. The salesperson there, a young lad, Tariq, greeted us enthusiastically.

When we asked him to demonstrate the features of a particular model of Apple Mac notebook, he first politely asked us what we knew about the Apple notebooks in general.

Realising our almost total ignorance on this subject, this young lad held us spellbound for the next twenty minutes, during which he displayed and demonstrated in a logical sequence almost all the features of the Apple notebook in superb fashion. He did it with the confident air of a skilled magician entertaining an audience by going through a well-practiced routine. **It seemed to us as though he had been born holding an Apple notebook in his hands.**

His knowledge was impeccable and his explanation and demonstration superb. When we asked him how he was so conversant with all these complex features, he replied that from his first three salaries, he ensured that he saved enough to buy an Apple notebook for himself, and that he knew the working of the piece inside out.

He said that if he was going to demonstrate and sell the piece to customers, his knowledge level of it needed to be absolute.

Hats off to him, and may he serve as a role model to other salespersons in that store.

It is possible to fly without motors, but not without knowledge and skill.

- Wilbur Wright

It is not that one is born possessing knowledge. It is not God's gift by default. It is acquired as a result of reading, observation, genuine interest and sincere, dedicated, organised, sustained efforts. And it is possible and indeed essential, to reach this level of knowledge in whichever area you as a salesperson have chosen to further your career.

Knowledge is power.

- Sir Francis Bacon

The Brains Trust Pearl:
No knowledge ever goes waste.

15

'Give more than you get',
is life's great golden rule

If you've yet to learn that,
then please go back to school

There is this very customer savvy ice-cream salesman attending the counter of a popular ice-cream store. He is the one for whom all the regular customers will wait in line to be served by. The secret of his popularity is supremely simple.

There is a fixed quantity of ice-cream which needs to be served in each cup or cone that a customer buys. This quantity is fixed by the management. The quantity is not in the hands of the salespersons at the counter to decide.

But while the **other ice-cream salesmen** in the parlour **carelessly** take a large scoop of ice cream, pile it into the cup or cone, and then proceed to scrape away the extra quantity; **this particular ice-cream salesman carefully** puts a small scoop of ice-cream in the cup or cone initially, examines the cup, and then **adds a little more** ice-cream to the cone or cup, ultimately bringing it to the same level that the other careless salesmen also do.

In both scenarios, the net amount of ice-cream served to the customer is the same, but the customer's perception in both cases is as different as chalk and cheese.

And as the saying goes – **The customer's perception is your reality.**

In the case of the salesmen who mindlessly put in a little more ice cream and then take it away, **the customer feels he is being cheated; being robbed.** The customer is already looking upon it as **HIS** ice cream from the moment it is put into the cup or the cone. But in the other scenario, the Super Salesman is looked upon as a benevolent Santa Claus.

The customer simply **CANNOT** enjoy the product or service when he feels the **slightest spark of injustice** or irritation with regards to it in his mind.

If the customer feels, for whatever reason, that he has got less from the transaction than he was given to expect, that's the beginning of the end of your relationship with him.

- Cyrus M Gonda, Dr. Kalim Khan

If for example, as an insurance salesperson, you did not inform your client when his premium was due, it's something which will rankle in his mind.

He will feel that it was his right to receive this service from you. No more business or referrals can be expected from him.

To truly appreciate and be able to implement this positive habit of 'Giving more than you get', you need to develop the habit of regularly performing little acts of kindness for people you know and meet. Once this habit is developed and ingrained in your system, it will stand you in good stead throughout your sales career.

You cannot live a perfect day without doing something for someone who will never be able to repay you.

- John Wooden

Give your customer that little bit extra – in terms of:

- Time
- Understanding
- Effort

It doesn't cost you the moon, but it repays dividends which you couldn't even begin to dream of.

The feeling that your customer gets when he receives that little extra need not be measurable in material or monetary terms. The little extra of yourself that you give will be returned to you with interest.

And if the returns are delayed, they will come to you with compound interest. And the returns will reach you in unexpected ways, from unexpected sources, time after time after time. It is a guarantee.

It is a law of nature, just as is the law of gravity.

Not only is it more blessed to give than to receive,
it also makes perfect business sense to do so.

- Cyrus M Gonda, Dr. Kalim Khan

It is not necessary that the scales need to fall in your favour after every single transaction. **In fact, if you attempt to extract the maximum from every transaction you undertake, the opposite party would constantly keep finding itself at the losing end.**

Needless to say, this would never result into a repeat customer being created or a referral being generated. And as we mentioned, business from repeat customers and referrals constitute your bread, butter, jam and cheese as a salesperson.

The most valuable extra that you can bestow on your customer is the priceless gift of your time.

All courtesies extended to him while on transaction, by itself are the biggest motivator for customer loyalty. These courtesies can only be extended if you don't aim to terminate a transaction as soon as possible, or attempt to conclude it within a limited time-span. It is very unfortunate that some organisations today actually measure the efficiency and productivity of their salespersons by calculating the time they take during a client meet, or on after sales-service, or in completing a transaction.

We very strongly advocate that any salesperson in any form of customer transaction must consciously spend a healthy amount of time with the customer, making the customer feel important.

We are sure you will agree that some of the best practitioners of the philosophy of giving that little extra are the **traditional Indian jewelry houses** who have understood the psyche of the Indian lady.

Look at the amount of time the salespersons in the best jewelry shops invest with their customers. The jewelers develop and strengthen the rapport by:

- Calling for a cup of tea or a soft drink depending on the weather
- Chatting with the lady about her family and the functions for which she is making the purchase
- Giving her extra plastic carry bags and calendars when she leaves the shop which she proudly carries away as hard won trophies

It is no wonder that these jewelry houses retain their customers, generation after generation after generation. That is why in Indian households, they are known as **The Family Jeweler.**

No person has ever been honoured for what he received.
Honour has been the reward for what he gave.

- Calvin Coolidge

The Brains Trust Pearl:
Whatever you give with your heart, comes back to you
with compound interest.

16

The strongest of us needs more than
two hands to achieve

What ten average men can do,
a giant may only conceive

In the process of selling any product or service, the salesperson may be the only individual who is visible to the customer at the front end. But there are many other departments and individuals involved in the culmination of the sales process.

The entire selling process will function better, the more there is:

- Regular interaction
- Positive feedback
- Strong rapport
- Open two way communication,

between all such departments and persons concerned.

It takes many, many individuals apart from the salesperson at the front end to make the sale happen and to keep the customer satisfied.

For example, in the armed forces, it is the brave men at the front-end who engage the enemy in battle, often sacrificing their lives in the process. But their supreme courage would have little impact on the outcome of the battle were it not for the men behind the front lines, who supported them by providing them with:

- Medical supplies
- Logistical support
- Uniforms
- Food and rations
- Equipment
- Transportation

The better that you as a salesperson understand your chain of support and the importance of the role of others in your organisation upon whom you depend for your success:

- The better will be your understanding of the constraints in which they operate
- The more improved will be your rapport with them
- And the more successful the salesperson you will ultimately become

One of us authors was once selected to undergo the prestigious two year induction as a trainee at the **Taj Mahal Hotel, Mumbai.** Our batch of eleven trainees had been selected with the objective of developing us as the potential general managers who would be handling the Taj Hotel properties across the country within the next ten years. During the course of the intensive induction, in-depth training was provided in diverse departments such as:

- Laundry
- Maintenance
- Security
- Kitchens
- Purchase

It was very clear that none of us would be working in any of these departments once our induction was complete. But the logic was crystal clear. The induction was preparing us to be general managers in the future. As general managers of the hotel, we could face situations where a guest complained about power failure in his room, or a stain on his laundered shirt, and so on.

It is not that we as general managers would have to personally restore electric supply, or remove the stain on the shirt. But we would have to know the back-end functioning of these support departments and would need to be in a good position to give accurate and effective answers to guest queries on the spot. Also the rapport we would have generated with the staff of the support departments during our induction would enable us to know the right person to speak to within that department, when the need arose in the future. In fact, throughout our induction, we were encouraged by the management to spend less time with our group of eleven, (with whom we had bonded), and spend more time interacting with and getting to know staff from all other departments.

Even in certain restaurants, the tips that are left by satisfied guests for the service staff are equally shared with the kitchen staff by the waiters at the end of the shift, as without the efforts of the kitchen staff, a tasty meal could never have been enjoyed by the guest at the table.

So:

- **Rambo**
- **The Lone Ranger**
- **The One Man Army**

may all be inspiring and entertaining tales, but they hardly do justice to the concept of teamwork.

For every hero in the fore-front, there are a hundred unsung heroes in the background, giving vital support. Remember, if any job, however insignificant it may appear to be, was not vitally important to the organisation, it would not have existed.

As someone rightly said – **There are no small jobs, there are only small men.**

The inventor genius, **Thomas Alva Edison,** was hardly the lone ranger that many of us believe him to be. The electric light bulb, for whose invention Edison is most remembered, was hardly his invention alone. He had a team of around thirty trained scientists and assistants, who worked round the clock in a state of the art laboratory, which itself was built with corporate funding.

The light bulb saw the light of day as a result of the work of a well knit team of:

- Mathematicians
- Engineers
- Glassblowers
- Chemists
- Physicists

Edison was the face of this superb team.

But he could never, ever, have achieved success by himself.

What set him apart from other inventors was his determination and drive; his love for continuous improvement in his chosen field, which is what all salespersons can learn to emulate.

> *Independent? We are all dependent on one another,*
> *every soul of us on earth.*

> - George Bernard Shaw

By focusing on the importance of teamwork, **in no way are we pulling down the importance of the individual.** Rather, **we are recognising and emphasising the importance of the individual as a vital member of a successful team.**

A true incident that **Dr. Hoshi Bhiwandiwala,** (considered to be the father of the field of Event Management in India), once witnessed and likes to often narrate, goes as follows.

A well known stage director, as renowned for the quality of his choreography as he was for his arrogant attitude towards his junior staff, was once staging a thriller play in front of an elite audience. During the practice session of that play the day before the actual performance, this director had yelled, screamed and abused a stage boy (whose job it was to pull the stage curtains open and shut at the appropriate times), for a minor lapse on his part. Now came the big day. The play was on. The audience watched enthralled, and the final sequence (a breathtaking one, painstakingly practiced), was fast approaching. The audience's eyes were riveted on the stage as the final sequence commenced, and then that seemingly unimportant stage boy, (who was apparently an 'insignificant' part of the team), and who had been humiliated by the mighty director a day before, 'accidentally' pulled the stage curtains shut, totally ruining the sequence and the entire evening for all concerned.

The director was livid, but the damage was done.

In similar vein, the salesperson too needs to remember that his success depends upon the efforts put in by his logistics people, his wholesaler, his distributor, his administration staff, his transporter, and endless others. The more quality time that he spends with them, the more will his relations with them solidify.

This will hugely help him achieve enhanced sales volumes and improve his relations with his customers by helping him deliver on the commitments he has made.

Just as a body cannot stand erect without a backbone, neither can a salesperson hold his head high without the solid support of his back-end team to support him.

- Cyrus M Gonda, Dr. Kalim Khan

A successful individual we know is employed in the field of advertisement sales with a television channel. He says that his clients, who advertise through him, regularly have urgent requirements, where they even contact him at midnight to telecast a certain advertisement the very next morning. Whereas salespersons from other channels often refuse such requests, as all channels require a twenty-four hour advance time period before they can telecast an advertisement, our friend manages to do the needful even at such short notice because he has developed an excellent rapport with the scheduling team in his own channel.

Due to this rapport, his scheduling team permits him this flexibility and helps him accomodate last minute client requests and they take care of his client's urgent telecast needs. Because he often helps out his clients in this manner, his clients give him a lot of extra business in appreciation. **Needless to say, he attributes a huge portion of his success to his excellent equation with the scheduling team of his own channel.**

There are parts of a ship, which taken by themselves, would sink. The engine would sink. The propeller would sink. But when these parts of a ship are built together, they float.

- Ralph Sockman

The Brains Trust Pearl:
Your strength and ability to serve your customer depends on the solid rapport you have developed and maintained with your back-end team.

17

There is no rule which exists
that says 'only one can win'

In business and in life,
putting down your rival is the only sin

The tendency to bad-mouth the competitor, or at least run down his product, service or even his character, is almost universal in appeal, whether in politics, or love, or even in business. But it is a tendency that can have negative repercussions for the transmitter.

Salespersons, especially inexperienced ones, tend to feel that it is easier to identify an outstanding negative in their competitor's product or service, rather than an outstanding positive in their own.

— Cyrus M Gonda, Dr. Kalim Khan

Through experience, we can state that it is the second route (identifying outstanding positives in your own brand), which brings a salesperson far superior results.

Every product or service has its own unique selling point or USP, else it could not have survived in the marketplace. Once that plus point has been identified and clearly understood, an increase in the salesperson's confidence in the product or service will be the logical by-product. This will automatically lead to a superior presentation by the salesperson to the prospect.

Negativism breeds negativism. By focusing on the negative attributes of the competitor's product or service, an overall attitude of negativity seeps into the personality of the salesperson. This will reflect in his:

- Words
- Expressions
- Body language

Then the natural cheery smile, so essential to the success of a salesperson, will be relegated into the background.

One man cannot hold another man down in the ditch
without remaining down in the ditch with him.

\- Booker T Washington

The presentation time that your prospect has gifted you is valuable. Use it positively and constructively. **If during your presentation, you dwell upon the negative aspects of your competitor's product, you will be implying to the prospect that your own product has very little worth fit to be projected.** It displays a lack of confidence in your own product. It is a mistake that could turn your prospects off faster than lightning. Yet it is an error that even experienced salespersons often tend to make.

Ponder on this. What do **YOU** feel about salespersons who approach you and waste your valuable time talking about their competitor's negative aspects?

You don't appreciate them, do you?

As a Super Salesperson, you must be extremely clear about the fact that the time your prospect has given you is to be invested productively. This time is to be used to highlight and project the advantages and benefits of **YOUR** brand.

The customer doesn't want to hear from you how bad your
competitor is. He wants to hear from you how good you are.

\- Cyrus M Gonda, Dr. Kalim Khan

As a salesperson that has the customer's best interests at heart, you ought to even recommend to him a competitor if you feel that your competitor can provide your customer what you cannot provide at this moment of time.

For example, at a particular bookstore, we heard the manager guiding a customer who wanted a particular book which this store didn't have in stock, to their competitor's store. Not only did the manager provide the customer the name of the competing bookstore, he also patiently gave the address and proper directions with landmarks to reach the same.

Such positive actions don't lose you a customer. In fact they gain the gratitude and the goodwill of the customer and help you develop a strong rapport with him.

Ultimately, what builds your reputation and what the customer remembers in such circumstances, is that you selflessly helped him out and that he got served through you as a medium. You will definitely get the reward for this generosity and large heartedness. The customer will definitely come to you in future when he knows that you can serve his requirements.

A light hearted story – A man had grown up not knowing who his father was. Now he was keen on finding out, but all research led to a dead end. His friend suggested that if he was really keen on finding out the identity of the paternal parent, the solution was simple. **All he had to do was contest elections and the opposition candidate would do the job for him.** This is because all that political candidates seem to do at election time is to run down their opponents. Rarely do they talk about their own strengths.

So now take a minute and think of the brands you respect and are in awe of. And then think of the brands you take casually. The difference between the two sets of brands would be – The brands you respect and are in awe of, never made attempts to put down their competitors. They provided clear cut demonstration through their products and services as to why they themselves were great.

This is why **Johnson and Johnson** and **Gillette** are a couple of our favourite brands. Their marketing thrust has always been on their USPs and product innovation. They have never bad mouthed their competitors, and this keeping in mind that both the brands have been in business for so long.

A similar case in point as far as Indian brands are concerned would be the **Tata Group of companies**, which has always propagated fair means in business practices and never attempted to run down their competitors. This is primarily what endears this group of companies to their customers.

At the other extreme are certain cola companies, which spend hard earned customer revenue to bad mouth the competitor's brand.

Let not him who is houseless pull down the house of another,
but let him work diligently and build one for himself, thus
by example assuring that his own shall be safe from violence
when built.

- Abraham Lincoln

The Brains Trust Pearl:
Never 'bad-mouth' your competitor in front of a customer. Rather, 'good-mouth' your own brand.

18

'Sell anything to anyone'?
In selling there can be no greater crime

If you proceed with this false motto,
your career won't be worth a dime

We commence the explanation of this couplet by asking the reader a very serious question.

For this question, we would require you to provide a very honest answer.

An honest answer not to us, or to the world, but to your own self.

The **question** is – **'Could YOU, in your role as a customer, (not as a salesperson), be persuaded by some highly persuasive individual to buy ANY and EVERY product or service on earth, whether or not you could need it or afford it'?**

Foolish question, isn't it?

We have yet to come across a single person whose answer to this ridiculous question was an honest **YES.**

Then what makes us think that a statement such as **'I can sell anything to anybody'**, makes any sense?

The only thing such a statement can do is to help us to identify a conman; a hit and run artist.

Rather, successful salespersons take pride in the fact that they can identify prospects that have a genuine **NEED** for the product or service they are offering, and then they craft their presentation to demonstrate how their product or service can cater to that genuine need.

Believe us, there are sufficient individuals and organisations that have a need for your product or service without you going out of your way to look for people to con. Otherwise, your product or service would not have been conceived in the first place.

The only thing you will earn by attempting to sell anything to anyone, is a bad name.

– Cyrus M Gonda, Dr. Kalim Khan

If you have followed the message of our other couplets and have done your homework well, it would not be difficult for you to identify prospects with genuine need.

The problem is, as salespersons seldom go beyond thinking and speaking of the **FEATURES** of their product or service offering, they will continue to assume that every human being on earth is a potential prospect for their product or service.

This is because when we think in terms of **FEATURES**, these are inherent to the product or service, and will remain the same in case of all prospects.

An aluminum body will remain an aluminum body will remain an aluminum body, irrespective of the individual you are demonstrating your product to.

The problem with features is, they are one size fits all.

But as a Super Salesperson, you are **NOT** selling one size fits all.

Even cricket bats and hockey sticks come in different sizes and qualities, and different people prefer to play different sports.

The key to successful salesmanship is to **MATCH** the product or service to the prospect.

For this, you need to understand your product or service from your **PROSPECT'S** perspective, and not your own.

Only then will you begin thinking in terms of **BENEFITS**, and not in terms of **FEATURES**.

Customers want to hear what **benefits** your product or service can provide them.

For example, leading hotels do **NOT** say – **We have comfortable beds.**

THAT would be a **feature.**

Rather, they would say – **We provide you with a sound night's sleep.**

Now **THAT** is a **benefit** which a customer is willing to pay a premium for.

And as we said, the best salespersons and organisations individually customise and craft their offerings to suit the tastes of individual customers.

So, rather than provide all customers with a standard pillow, the **Devi Garh Hotel** in **Udaipur** offers its guests the pillow of their choice.

It provides a '**Pillow Menu**' in each room.

The various pillows it offers are:

- **Cuddled Micro Fibre Pillow** (Feature) – Designed to create a genuine and sensual feeling of being held or cuddled (Benefit)
- **Natural Silk Cotton Pillow** (Feature) – Radiates a sense of tranquility and calmness to generate a bonding between you and the natural bay windows (Benefit)
- **Slim Siliconized Hollow Fiber Pillow** (Feature) – Allows you to maintain a straight posture, yet safe and eliminates any discomfort to the user (Benefit)
- **Firm Siliconized Hollow Fiber** (Feature) – For those who prefer a firm and controlled feeling and to keep the neck angle firm (Benefit)
- **Standard Polly Fils Micro Fiber** (Feature) – For those with any allergy to synthetic material (Benefit)

The list goes on.

For the customer friendly Devi Garh Hotel, one size definitely does **NOT** fit all.

We also strongly advocate that a salesperson sit across the table with his client not to just present and speak, but more importantly to **listen and observe**.

There is ample proof today which shows that **pushing a product never works.**

For one, customers have become smarter.

And second, your customer depends upon your expertise, just as a patient depends upon a doctor for expert advice, to help him make a suitable medical decision. Your job as a salesperson is not to simply push a product of which you as a salesperson have excess stock, which you want to get rid off at any cost. **If you genuinely act as a trusted adviser,** customers will stay with you for a lifetime and recommend you to everyone possible.

Just calculate which is more beneficial for you as a salesperson – One hit and run sale, or a lifetime of referrals.

Don't make your clients purchase goods which you know will not satisfy them or be suitable for their needs. This will only succeed in creating post-purchase dissonance.

The customer will always vouch for the salesperson who takes the time and effort to understand his unique needs. Treat every customer as though he is unique in the world.

He actually **IS** unique.

And so are you.

This is why you cannot and should not attempt to sell anything to anyone.

In a restaurant we once visited, along with our meal we ordered a bottle of mineral water. The manager who was taking our order politely told us –

"Sir, just for your information, the water we would anyway serve free of cost to you is already purified and very safe to drink. If you still wish to order a bottle of mineral water, let me know. But I would not want you to spend money unnecessarily."

This apparently trivial statement of his gave us a lot of faith about the quality of ingredients he used for preparing meals. It sent across a very strong signal that this man would not attempt to sell anything to anyone. From this, we also concluded that he would not cut corners on **ANY** issue concerning quality. His philosophy clearly was not to make as much money in as short a time as possible, but more importantly to maximise revenue by looking after the customer's interests.

We are now regular patrons at that restaurant.

The father of one of the authors, Cyrus, is a trusted adviser with the **Life Insurance Corporation of India** since over fifty years. When his clients approach him for advice on their insurance investments, he thoroughly studies and understands their needs before he makes any suggestions. And if as per his understanding, if at that moment of time, his client would be better off by investing his money not in insurance, but in another option such as fixed deposits or mutual funds which would suit their current purpose better, he honestly tells them so.

At that moment, he definitely appears to 'lose' business, but his clients are so grateful for his honest advice and guidance, and place such implicit faith in him for his integrity and professional expertise and unbiased judgment, that when in future they or their family members or their friends **DO** have a genuine need for insurance, he is the only advisor they can think of and recommend.

The Brains Trust Pearl:
Guide your customers to make the right purchase decision and they will reward you with sufficient business for a lifetime.

19

A 'No' is sometimes said in anger,
a 'No' is sometimes said in pain

Do not take it to heart and person;
whistle, move on, try again

If you are going through hell, keep going.

- Winston Churchill

As a salesperson, it is good to practice listening to the word 'No'.

This message is not meant to dishearten you, but it needs to be understood in a positive context.

Life, especially for a salesperson, cannot always be a bed of roses.

And sometimes we may hit a lean patch for no fault of our own.

A series of No's may sometimes come our way.

Fine.

It happens to all of us.

This is the time to remind yourself that the darkest hour always lies before the dawn.

Do **NOT** make the fatal mistake of taking rejection of your product or service as a rejection of you as a person.

As **Sylvester Stallone** says, **"I take rejection as someone blowing a bugle in my ear to wake me up and get going, rather than retreat."**

Remember, if your system of selling is in place, if you have imbibed the attributes we have outlined in this book, if you possess within you the **Super Salesperson's Skill Set** (Copyright - Brains Trust Management Consultancy), if the qualities essential for success in the noble profession of selling have been acquired by you through methodical practice, then this series of **No's** will be a mere hiatus, only a temporary pause in your career.

If your system of selling is in place, you will soon be amply rewarded by the success that awaits all hard working, smart working and honest salespersons. But when you hear a 'No', it is important to keep your chin up and not lose confidence in yourself and in your abilities.

A rejection is nothing more than a necessary step in the pursuit of success.

- Bo Bennett

There are reasons outside your control and your sphere of goodness due to which a 'No' may sometimes come your way.

What you **SHOULD** be striving for is to develop the necessary attributes of the Super Salesperson, so that you need never listen to a 'No' from a customer for reasons which are **WITHIN** your control.

(For example; reaching late for an appointment, not having done your homework in terms of product knowledge well, and so on.) **Such reasons for losing a sale would be a criminal lapse on your part.**

As we said, there are multiple reasons for which a prospect may say a 'No', and many of these have nothing to do with your goodness as a salesperson.

For example:

- The prospect may be in a foul mood for a reason which has nothing to do with you
- He may not be in a frame of mind to appreciate the goodness and value of your offering
- Your offering may not suit his immediate requirement
- Your offering may not fit his current budget
- A competing product may be providing a feature and benefit which better suits his specific needs

As you can see, there is quite a long list.

But what you **CAN** and **SHOULD** do is learn from the 'No'.

That is very important.

And that learning is entirely within your control.

It is this learning which makes the 'No' worthwhile.

Analyse the reasons for the 'No'.

This analysis is essential to ensure continuous improvement in your:

- Sales methodology and approach
- Your presentation technique
- Your level of flexibility and adaptation to client needs
- Your listening skills
- Your sense of timing
- Your understanding of customer needs and customer behaviour
- Your knowledge of your products and your services

And so on.

Do not let a series of No's upset you.

Success in selling does not follow a mathematical pattern.

It is not always three No's followed by a Yes.

Each prospect and each sales call is separate from every other.

If your focus and approach is short term, then a single 'No' may affect your psyche.

You need to develop a larger vision to identify and learn from the 'No', as to what you can now do to ensure that more prospects frequent your brand.

Focusing on **WHY** you did not achieve your short term sales target is as ridiculous as asking a bus conductor, "How come so few passengers sat in your bus during this particular trip?"

You can't drag more people from other modes of transport and seat them in your bus and sell them tickets for the privilege.

Passengers **WILL** come.

Provided you improve your sales offering in areas of punctuality and frequency of service, enhance comfort levels, ensure customers are treated politely and courteously, and so on.

Enhancement of revenue and profitability will be the by-product of a methodical sales and service process. This will happen within a short period of time, once you set your system in place.

The problem is not with failure.

It can never be.

The best people on earth have faced failure.

The **problem** is that most people in general, and many salespersons in particular, **refuse to FAIL INTELLIGENTLY.**

Charles Kettering, the famed inventor, explained why it is **important** for us to 'Fail Intelligently'.

Kettering said – **"We need to teach the highly educated person that it is not a disgrace to fail, and that he must analyse every failure to find its cause. He must learn how to fail intelligently, for failing is one of the greatest arts in the world."**

Kettering provided the following suggestions in order to turn failure into success.

- Honestly face defeat, never fake success
- Exploit the failure, don't waste it. Learn all you can from it
- Never use failure as an excuse for not trying again

From Kettering, we learn that failure is an important part of life on the path to progress and success.

And finally, remember, you may feel **Thomas Edison and his team** failed multiple times while attempting to invent the light bulb. But they didn't 'fail' nine thousand times at making a light bulb. They learnt nine thousand ways how not to make a light bulb. And this learning was essential to their ultimate success.

Similarly, learn from the 'No' as to how not to be faced with a 'No' for that reason ever again in future.

Rejection is fun when you can learn from it and grow as a wiser person.

- Augie

The Brains Trust Pearl:

Develop the inner strength to withstand a 'No'. Learn from a 'No' rather than be disheartened by it. Moving from 'NO' to 'KNOW' should be your motto.

20

But should you try to be too pushy,
folks away from you will run

Selling then is never easy,
selling then is never fun

A salesperson definitely needs to develop the quality of persistence. It is essential to his success.

But being persistent is not the same as being pushy.

If the two terms meant the same thing, we would not have had two separate entries for them in the dictionary.

We would prefer to define **persistent** as – **Logically finishing what you have begun; not letting go half way, carrying the activity forward to its logical conclusion; letting go once you feel the end has been reached.**

Being persistent (and not pushy), will ensure that you do not spoil relations with prospects which could generate good business and positive recommendations in the future.

Pushy, on the other hand means .... Well, we've all experienced pushy people.

They're the ones whose calls we don't pick up, and whom we cross the street to avoid when we see them from far away.

Being pushy is a trait which results into Lose-Lose situations.

Being pushy in sales is like axing your own foot.

It is like digging your own grave.

Yet it is surprising to see how many salespersons feel that being pushy is the one thing necessary to succeed in sales.

There is nothing worse than aggressive stupidity.

- Johann Wolfgang von Goethe

No instance can better demonstrate what the term **pushy** exactly means when associated with the sales profession, than the following one narrated to us by an acquaintance.

Our friend, a young lady, had been invited to attend the meeting of a Network Marketing Company. (This company has now ceased to exist.)

She had been reluctant to attend the meeting as there was an attendance fee of Rupees Five Hundred involved, but she had been repeatedly told that attending this meeting would change her entire life.

"Even if you have a meeting scheduled with the President of the United States, cancel it, but attend this meeting", is what she was told.

She reluctantly agreed, as it was a friend who was inviting her to attend. She clarified at that stage itself that if there was any further investment required from her end once she attended the meeting, she was not in any position to invest, as she was about to get married, and she and her fiancé were saving all their money for their wedding day and their future life together. She was again assured that this meeting was life changing. "Just attend. Get your fiancé along."

She and her fiancé attended the meeting, which was addressed by a hyper-motivated, pushy individual. This man commenced the meeting by asking –

"How many of you in the audience can read from right to left?"

When everyone responded that they did their reading from left to right, (as is normal with the English and Indian scripts), he said he would prove them wrong.

He proceeded to do so. "When you visit a restaurant and pick up the menu, what do you read first? The item on the right hand side, which is the price tag for the dish. Only if it fits your budget would you proceed to the left hand column to see what dish the price tag represents. **So ladies and gentlemen, if you invest in our network marketing company, you will truly be able to read from left to right, without any concern for the price tag. Wouldn't you all like that?"**

He then proceeded to invite some young children of the audience members present onto the stage. He asked them what they would all like to be when they grew up. Some cute little kids said that they would like to become doctors or engineers or take up similar vocations. Again the man on the stage said to them-

"That's very nice, but education is expensive. Do you think your parents can afford to pay the fees on their current salary?"

Then he would address the audience and tell them that they would have no such worries if they invested in his company. Money would then flow like water.

Many audience members were already beginning to get turned off by this aggressive and pushy presentation.

The story doesn't end here.

Once a few more aggressive comments were made, the presentation was complete. Now a company manager was assigned to each audience member to convince them to invest and become agents of the company.

They were bluntly told –

"You will not get time to think this offer over. You cannot go home and discuss this offer with your families. This is your last chance to become a millionaire. We do not want people investing with us if they don't have faith in us. That is why we have told you to carry along your cheque book or your credit cards. Sign up now as we will never accept you as a member from tomorrow onwards."

Most people from the audience left as they did not like the fact that they were not even being given the opportunity to think the offer over.

Our lady friend and her fiancé were quietly about to leave, when a manager from the company cornered them and asked them why they were losing out on such a fantastic opportunity. The fiancé tactfully mentioned that since they were shortly to get married, they were saving all their money for their marriage day. The manager then geared up to top gear pushy salesmanship. Speaking to the man, he said –

"Imagine if this girl is kidnapped tomorrow, and the kidnappers ask for a ransom of Rupees Fifty Thousand. Would you not organise the money from somewhere? Where there is a will, there is a way."

The man then said that they had recently invested all their funds in a house and had even taken a housing loan which they had to repay.

"Wonderful", was the reply. **"Put your house on mortgage, raise the money and invest it in our firm."**

The couple walked away as fast as they could.

Incidentally, a couple of months after this incident, this Network Marketing Company folded up; taking with it the money which a few trusting people had invested.

Be persistent with your processes, rather than being pushy with your prospects.

- Cyrus M Gonda, Dr. Kalim Khan

The Brains Trust Pearl:
Do NOT push your products and services. Instead, learn the art of magnetically pulling customers towards your products and services.

21

Feet be quick but mind be quicker,
this will make order books thicker

With fast mind and faster wit,
your sales career will be a hit

We are always advised to be constantly active. But 'active' is a misleading word.

Running aimlessly around a tree, faster and faster, till you exhaust yourself and collapse, can definitely be considered as **activity**. But whether it can be classified as **productivity,** is a different question altogether.

As a salesperson who is always fighting against paucity of time, the thing to do is to channelise your effort, time and energy in the right direction so that you are productive, and not merely active.

To ensure that this happens – **It is your mind which ought to rule your feet.**

Strengthen your mind.

Just as we visit the gym to improve and strengthen our physique, our mind too needs to be regularly exercised in order for it to function at peak efficiency. There are many ways to achieve mental agility.

Some people enjoy reading.

Some solve intricate puzzles.

Some play word-games such as 'Scrabble.'

We know an **enthusiastic canteen boy** in the office of **The Hindu** newspaper, who creates crossword puzzles in his spare time which are published in his hometown newspaper in the state of Kerala.

The brain, like any other organ, needs exercise. It is calculated that an **average individual utilises a maximum of five percent of the potential brain power he possesses during his lifetime.** The balance ninety-five percent goes unutilised as the brain is not exercised on a regular basis.

The advantages of a sharp brain are multiple, especially in the sales profession:

- It increases your attention span and helps you focus on what the prospect is saying
- It keeps you sufficiently agile to look out for the subtle signs and hidden hints in the prospect's communication, which you can use to your advantage
- It enhances your vocabulary and helps you use the right word at the right time, thus creating a positive impact on the prospect
- Most important of all, it enables you to get into the habit of quick thinking, and turning a potentially disastrous situation into sales victory. This will be the result of quick wit on your part, which will impress the prospect. But take care that this wit and humour you use should be pleasant and gentle, used for positive purposes, and never with the intention of sarcasm

The **comedians who entertain us on stage** with their humorous one-liners are not born with the gift. They work hard at being funny. Being funny is very serious work.

These comedians read, they research, they explore tons of material and they practice and improve their routines till they're satisfied. The result of all this hard work is a happy and delighted audience, which comes back for more.

You too, have it in you, to impress your prospects with wit and gentle humour, resulting in large orders coming your way.

We would like to give just a couple of examples of actual sales situations, where quick thinking salespersons turned potential sales failure into stunning sales success.

One such example follows.

A team of finance sales professionals we know, once had an appointment with a very high net-worth client who was considering investing a huge sum of money through a financial institution. Many leading financial institutions were vying for this prestigious client. This team of finance professionals included a lady who was introduced to the client.

The client was told – **"Sir, this lady will handle your investments."**

The client immediately retorted – **"You expect a female to handle my investments?"**

Immediately the leader of the sales team, realising that the client had little faith in a female as far as financial knowledge was concerned, rectified the situation.

He intervened saying – "Of course what we meant was that she will be handling the **DEBT** component of your investment (the debt component carries no risk, and is relatively easy to handle.) This gentleman will handle the **EQUITY** (the risky part) of your investment."

Naturally, the deal was immediately secured.

Often the truth spoken with a smile will penetrate the mind and reach the heart, the lesson strikes home without wounding because of the wit in the saying.

- Horace

Another example of quick wit combined with linguistic expertise comes next.

An insurance salesperson had managed to sell individual policies to three individuals who were all partners of a partnership firm. He also had a policy which had been specifically designed for the benefit of partners of a partnership firm which he wanted these partners to jointly purchase, but they didn't seem interested.

In normal circumstances, when one of the partners of a partnership firm passes away, his wife would inherit the share of his partnership.

If she remarried, her new husband could become a partner of the firm by default, and he could be a person whom the original partners may not wish to work in partnership with, but they would have no choice.

A unique feature of the policy this salesperson was offering was that in the event of one of the partners passing away, the surviving partners would have first preference in taking over the partnership, rather than the deceased partner's wife, which is normally the case. This was a feature, which thought the salesman, if worded intelligently, would strike a chord in the minds of the partners. This is how he put it to each partner. –

"In case your partner passes away, and his wife who inherits his share of her deceased husband remarries, **how would you like to be the partner of your partner's widow's second husband, when you don't know who that person could be?"**

He identified a unique need, worded it intelligently to create impact, and made his sale.

It is by vivacity and wit that man shines in company.

- Lord Chesterfield

In the following humorous sales situation, quick wit saved embarrassment.

A person walked into a grocery store, asking for half a head of lettuce. The salesperson went into the inner room and told the manager – **"There's an idiot who wants to buy half a head of lettuce."**

Turning around, he saw the customer had followed him into the inner room and heard every word he had just said. Without a pause, the salesperson continued – **"And this nice gentleman would like to purchase the other half."**

The monuments of wit and learning are more durable than the monuments of power, or of the hands.

- Unknown

The Brains Trust Pearl:
Take time and effort to sharpen your mind. It is your greatest asset.

22

Your customers are many,
they come in every shape and size

The salesperson who doesn't judge them,
will walk off with the prize

Negatively pre-judging the purchase ability and intention of a prospect is one of the most common, and also probably the most fatal error that salespersons tend to make.

We recently met a friend of ours, and admired the Rolex wrist watch he had on. "Must have cost quite a bit", we said.

"Around three lakh rupees", was the reply, accompanied with a broad smile on his handsome face.

We asked him where he had purchased it from.

His smile immediately narrowed into a frown, as if recalling an unpleasant memory.

We repeated our question, and this is the answer we got.

He said there was quite a story behind this purchase.

(Let us add at this stage that although our friend is fond of and can afford the best brands of accessories, he tends to be slightly shabby in his attire and in his overall appearance.)

He said that once he had made up his mind to purchase a Rolex, he visited an elite store which stocked exclusive brands of watches. He entered the store, and was looked upon by the sales staff inside as though he were a piece of rubbish that had floated in with the passing wind. The sales attendant he approached didn't even greet him. Instead, he had almost an arrogant sneer on his face.

He literally behaved as though he were just about tolerating our friend's presence in the store. Our friend had to repeat his request at least thrice before the attendant grudgingly took out a watch which our friend wished to see from the display window. All this while, the arrogant sneer was plastered on the salesperson's face.

Our friend walked out of this 'elite' store in disgust.

He immediately visited another showroom in the same locality which also stocked these exclusive and expensive time pieces.

The response in this second store was fantastic:

- Our friend was greeted and treated as though he were a VIP
- The sales attendants were extremely attentive, (that's where the word 'attendant' comes from)
- They promptly displayed all the watches our friend desired to see
- They politely and knowledgeably explained the features of each watch model they displayed
- They served him a cool drink

In short, the salespersons behaved as though he were already a regular customer, having given them huge volumes of business in the past, when in fact he was visiting this store for the first time.

Our friend purchased his Rolex from this store. (The same model of Rolex he purchased here, he had also seen at the first store he had visited.)

Not only that, he also purchased an expensive spectacle frame from the spectacle showroom next door, which also was a sister concern of this watch store.

Sometimes, when the salespersons in one store are rude, and in the next store they are polite, the customer makes a purchase from the second store primarily to vent his frustration at the attitude displayed by the attendants in the first store.

A pilot friend of ours, who frequently visits Europe, mentions that he is sometimes looked down upon when he enters elite luxury stores, as though he were just browsing and couldn't afford to buy anything the store had to offer. He mentions that in such situations, he casually opens his wallet and displays a huge volume of high denomination currency notes to the salespersons in these stores. Their attitude towards him immediately changes, but by then it is a little too late.

The wise man never trusts in appearances.

- Confucius

Never pre-judge or behave arrogantly and half-heartedly with customers. Customers can immediately sense this attitude.

When you as a salesperson are stressed or overworked, it is especially probable that such negative behaviour may unknowingly occur. Keep an eye open for such situations, and if possible, take a short break and de-stress yourself.

Many years ago, we used to spend quite some time at a friend's bookstore. We and the store owner often used to play a behavioural game. We used to try evaluating from a customer's appearance, approach and body language as to whether he would buy or had merely come to browse. After we had made our quick individual evaluations, we laid small, silent bets with each other based on our evaluations. Many times, each of us, (including the store owner), was so confident when we laid our bets, but we turned out to be blatantly incorrect, and received metamorphic slaps on our faces. **Often, a customer that one of us had pre-decided as having no purchase potential, walked off with books and magazines worth thousands, without even haggling for a discount.**

One particular incident we had in that store stands out in memory. It involved a college going teenage boy, who asked to be shown an expensive foreign car magazine. He was ignored, as our friend, the store owner, felt that the boy had come to the store to while away his time. The boy turned out to be the son of a college librarian and this college was currently giving this bookstore a huge volume of business, to the tune of lakhs of rupees a year. The boy later mentioned to his father, (the college librarian), about the shabby treatment he had been given here. The father almost stopped college purchases from that store. Our friend had to perform heavy duty damage control to retain this customer with his bookstore.

Once we negatively pre-decide a prospect's purchase intentions and appoint ourselves as judge, jury and executioner rolled into one, we start on the path to arrogance and become indifferent in our sales approach.

\- Cyrus M Gonda, Dr. Kalim Khan

And if we continue this pre-judging activity on a regular basis, it becomes a habit, and this undesirable attribute becomes part of the personality, and will be displayed even while interacting with genuine customers.

This stage marks the beginning of the end of an otherwise promising sales career.

Never ever grudge a customer or look down upon him simply because he spends a long time in browsing.

We have even had the fan above our heads switched off while we have been browsing at certain outlets as a signal for us that we have browsed too long; now it is time to buy or to leave. Inevitably, when forced into such a choice, we leave.

The first stage to shopping is through window shopping.

\- Cyrus M Gonda, Dr. Kalim Khan

The Brains Trust Pearl:
Judge your customers at your own risk.

23

Understanding your customer,
is the single biggest thing

If this is what you're good at,
soon you'll rise from Jack to King

A few decades ago, the concept of 'Intelligence Quotient' or IQ, was given prime importance when selecting applicants for jobs. The assumption being that the most intelligent individual would automatically turn out to be the most productive and valuable employee.

Today, the concept of 'Emotional Quotient' or EQ, has far outstripped the concept of IQ in importance.

While intelligence is fine, desirable, necessary and even an essential attribute that a Super Salesperson needs to possess, it ranks a little lower on the scale as compared with the almost divine attribute of true understanding.

\- Cyrus M Gonda, Dr. Kalim Khan

Organisations today realise that customers prefer to deal with salespersons that can understand them, empathise with them and their innermost feelings, insecurities and emotions.

In fact, the 'E' in the term EQ could very well stand for the word **Empathy.** All great and lasting relationships are built on the foundation stone of understanding.

A sense of oneness and unity evolves when two entities, whether they are individuals or mighty nations, find common ground by taking the time and effort to understand each other. The result of course, of such understanding, is mutual benefits for both sides.

\- Cyrus M Gonda, Dr. Kalim Khan

The following is a lovely tale containing a wealth of meaning for all salespersons to imbibe.

Before I can sell John Smith
What John Smith buys,
I have to begin to see John Smith
Through John Smith's eyes

A sign in a pet store mentioned that some puppies were for sale. A young boy, John Smith by name, slowly walked into the store and handed over a five dollar note to the owner, saying – "I'd like to buy a puppy, please."

The owner replied – "I'm sorry son, but these puppies are a special breed and very expensive. Each puppy costs a hundred dollars."

John was disappointed, but asked if he could have a look at the puppies. He offered to pay a dollar for the privilege. The owner smiled and told John that there was no charge for merely looking at them. The owner whistled, and from the back of the store came trotting the mother dog, with four little puppies running behind her. And later came a puppy four or five paces behind its brothers and sisters, limping and struggling to keep up with the rest.

The boy pointed to the limping puppy and said excitedly – "This is the puppy I want to buy."

The owner told him – "You wouldn't want that puppy. Our veterinarian says she was born without a hip socket, and will never be able to run, jump, and do all the other fun things that boys and puppies like to do as they grow up together."

John gazed at the pet shop owner, pulled up his own trouser legs, and displayed the heavy steel braces on either side of his legs, joined together with leather caps over the knees. John suffered from the effects of polio, and as he pointed at his own legs, he told the pet shop owner – "**I can't run or jump either. I need that puppy because I know she'll be able to relate to me the way I would be able to relate to her. That puppy is just the right one for me. This is the puppy I want to buy because she would suit me the best.** I'll pay you five dollars now and five dollars a week till I've paid you the hundred dollars."

Before I can sell John Smith

What John Smith buys,

I have to begin to see John Smith

Through John Smith's eyes

In the beginning of the month of March of a particular year not long ago, a lady salesperson representing an organisation that is into financial research and selling of financial databases of organisations approached our Management Institute to demonstrate her organisation's product. The product was an amazing databank, a literal boon for MBA students specialising in the field of finance, as it contained all possible industry-wise financial information of a huge number of companies. The utility of this database was beyond question, and we were more than willing to purchase the package and we also conveyed this to the salesperson. Having said that, we realised that purchasing this particular database in the month of March did not make any sense to us as customers for two reasons.

One – This package had an annual renewal charge of approximately Rupees Four and a Half Lakhs per annum.

Two – April, May and June are three months in any Management Institute in Mumbai when there are no students are on campus, so **the package would be lying idle for three months if it was purchased immediately.** The month of July would have been an ideal time for purchase from the Institute's point of view.

Hence, we decided to purchase this package in July, so as to increase utility for us in terms of students using the product to its optimum.

In spite of conveying our viewpoint, the lady salesperson was hell-bent on insisting that this purchase be done immediately, that is, in March. She in fact followed up and called to the extent of harrowing us to ensure that the sale took place in the month of March. It is only when we put our foot down firmly and confronted her on her incessant follow-up, that she revealed that **her annual incentives were at stake if the sale did not take place in the month of March that year**.

This was outrageous. And the nonsense just does not stop there. While we stuck to our guns and did not purchase in March, there was no follow-up from her end or from her organisation thereafter, ever. When they did not bother to get in touch with us in July as we had requested them to, we did not bother to get in touch with them either. We identified and purchased a competing product which also met our needs.

The organisation and the lady salesperson lost a definite sale which could have happened in July, simply because they did not understand the unique and valid requirements of the customer. **Rather, they were in the pursuit of a blind sale at a time which was CONVENIENT FOR THEM AS SALESPERSONS, to meet their annual March ending targets.**

The ability to see the situation as the other side sees it is one of the most important skills a negotiator can possess.

- Roger Fisher, William Ury

The Brains Trust Pearl:
Every customer you serve is a unique human being. Take time and effort to understand him as an individual. He will love you for it. And he will reward you for it as well.

24

Only of 'I', 'Me', 'Myself', alone;
please do not ever think

At any cry or call for help,
please do rush without a blink

In the entire process of selling, the function of **After Sales Service** (a very vital function), **is too often given step motherly treatment.**

But the attention paid by salespersons to this crucial function is what makes customers loyal, secures you repeat sales, and assures you of a regular stream of revenue.

The most respected, trusted and highly sought after doctors are the ones who can always be relied on to rush to their patient's side in an emergency. This is the reason why the medical profession is also known as the noble profession. They put the patient's comfort and convenience foremost, ahead of their own personal comfort and convenience.

In fact, every doctor takes an oath that he will do this.

You too, as a salesperson, can take such an oath and practice it.

Not only does it make you feel proud about your profession, it builds your reputation as a concerned and caring salesperson, and is great for business as well.

After sales service, a period of time when the customer needs you the most, is equally, if not more important, than pursuing new sales.

- Cyrus M Gonda, Dr. Kalim Khan

We have already spoken about the importance that customer retention plays in developing you into a Super Salesperson. Too often, we have encountered salespersons who are attentiveness personified, till the time they receive the purchase order in their hand. Then they disappear, not even bothering to receive the customer's calls post-sale. Such salespersons lose all opportunities for referrals and all future sales opportunities from this customer due to their unprofessional approach.

This is such a pity, because in order to get the sale, they have proved that they possess the ability to be good salespersons, and they shift their approach once the sale is secured.

The following true episode we were privileged to hear about from the salesperson himself, would further enlighten you as to how this attribute can be practiced and how rewarding it can be for you to emulate this level of dedication.

While we were conducting a Customer Service Workshop for the managers of **Emerson** (the world's leading Uninterrupted Power Supply provider), a senior manager of the company narrated how he personally went above and beyond the call of duty to ensure customer satisfaction.

This is what he told us.

Late one night when the rain was pouring down, this manager's elderly father was suddenly taken unwell. He was coughing severely and the manager was doing his best to make him comfortable. At that time, he received a call from a customer, frantically saying that the UPS in his office was not functioning and needed immediate servicing, else valuable data would be lost. (Emerson, being in the field where twenty four hour service is essential, their sales and service engineers were on call around the clock.)

This manager tried to get in touch with his colleague, who didn't pick up his phone as he was apparently sleeping.

With his father still very ill and the rain having increased in intensity, the manager stoically got dressed and was about to leave for the customer's office premises, when he attempted to wake his colleague one last time. Fortunately, this time he got through, and his colleague attended to the customer in his place.

Around ten days after this incident, the customer who had made the frantic call met this manager and asked him – "While I was speaking to you the other night about my UPS problem, I could hear someone coughing very severely in the background at your residence. At that time, I didn't give it much thought, as I was too concerned with my own problem. I hope everything is fine."

The Emerson manager thanked the customer for his concern and explained that it had been his father who had been extremely unwell and he had in fact passed away a couple of days later.

The customer was extremely apologetic and highly appreciative that in spite of such an adverse situation, the manager had still been willing to come over to his assistance. The customer stated –

"My faith in Emerson to help me out during emergencies has just gone up a hundred fold."

Every relationship requires sacrifice.

- Unknown

At this juncture, we would like to put in a word to organisations about the importance of employee retention and about generating a sense of belongingness and loyalty among employees towards the organisation.

No organisation has a right to expect a high level of commitment from its employees in terms of going the extra mile for its customers, if the organisation itself does not initiate this level of commitment and support towards its own staff in the first place.

And a message for those salespersons who feel that the customer's problems are the customer's headaches. We sincerely believe – **Something which you feel is not your problem, but you feel is only your customer's problem, is in reality your problem.**

We learned a fantastic example of putting the customer first from the staff of the organisation – **Burgmann India Ltd.** It is an engineering company, manufacturing and selling valves and seals to factories and plants. This is how the story goes.

There was a huge refinery which was currently a client of Burgmann's competitior. One evening, a day before Christmas, a seal in this refinery malfunctioned, causing stoppage of work. It was a humongous seal, weighing over a ton.

Burgmann's competitors, who had sold the seal to this refinery, were neither able to service it nor replace it with immediate effect.

A Burgmann sales representative, who was fortunately in that refinery at that time, making a sales presentation, became aware about this and saw it as a fantastic opportunity to serve and wow the prospect.

He co-ordinated with his own organisation (Burgmann), identified that they had a similar seal in stock and assured the manager of the refinery that if given an opportunity, they would replace the seal within twenty four hours. The desperate refinery manager gave him a go ahead, as his work had stopped till the seal could be replaced.

The Burgmann sales and service team hired a helicopter and had the gigantic seal air-lifted to the refinery. The salesperson and two service engineers from Burgmann went along and ensured that the seal was installed and functional by putting in fifteen solid hours of work without a rest break. The salesperson and one of the service engineers from Burgmann who achieved this task were Catholics, and both worked the entire day of Christmas, staying away from their homes and their families on this important family occasion, but ensured client delight. The client was so thrilled, that a huge chunk of business came Burgmann's way from that refinery within a short span of time.

Without selfless service, no one ever receives the fruits of their rewards.

- Sri Guru Granth Sahib

As a wise man once said – **The wise man puts himself last, and in doing so, he puts himself first.**

The Brains Trust Pearl:
Selfless service is the key to sales success.

25

Make a sale once, make a sale twice;
after that you've made a friend

In your sales career that's important,
that's what matters in the end

It has been rightly observed by **Peter Drucker,** the undisputed Management Guru of the twentieth century, that the **primary objective of any business ought to be Customer Retention.** In other words, creating a customer for life.

This is because it is only regular, repeat customers, who bring about regular, repeat business, which in turn is capable of generating the volumes of revenue that can ensure business survival and sustain business growth.

Also, there is a huge cost in terms of time, money and effort which goes into convincing a new, prospective customer to deal with you as an individual salesperson and also as an organisation.

This huge cost is entirely eliminated when it comes to dealing with retained customers, as they don't need to be convinced of keeping you on as their regular service provider if their past experiences with you have been positive.

It is a globally established fact that approximately eighty percent of the volume of business in any industry comes from approximately twenty percent of the client base, which constitutes the retained customers.

These are the customers who have tried and tested your products and your services and feel comfortable with the same. They are now your friends.

These are the customers you need to concentrate your efforts on, as they are a great source of further business potential and referrals.

It is always better to dig for gold or oil where you are sure it exists, rather than cold call at random locations. Not that new leads don't need to be generated, but not at the cost of ignoring the existing client base and their needs, both material as well as emotional.

All friendships are primarily strengthened by regularly keeping in touch. Think of all your old friends. The ones you are close to are the ones you communicate with on a regular basis. So the best thing you can do to maintain your Key Accounts is to be in regular touch with them.

Don't be a Santa Claus and connect with them just once a year when you need business.

- Remember their birthdays
- Remember their anniversaries
- Remember their wife's birthdays and subtly remind them of the same in case they have forgotten. They will be eternally grateful

Previously in this book, we mentioned about the father of one of the authors of the 'Song of the Super Salesperson', who is in the field of insurance.

He has been in the field of Insurance for over 50 years but when he started he made it a point not to approach any close friends or relatives for seeking insurance business has he thought that any such sale would be not because of his competence but on other grounds. He says that most of the insurance business secured was of those who were total strangers, who subsequently became closely acquainted. Most of the insurance business secured was referred by existing clients. In fact, a number of them approached him for further insurance instead he approaching them.

Unlike most insurance advisers today, who fail to retain a client even for a period of a year, **Minoo R Gonda has FOURTH GENERATION CLIENTS. He has insured the great-grandchildren of the clients he had initially developed when he started off as an insurance advisor, over fifty years ago.**

The level of service he provides is so impeccable, that one of his clients who was shifting to another city told him, **"I wish you would also set up an agency in that city. I'll be lost without you."**

In fact, the Managing Director of the Life Insurance Corporation, on hearing of his fantastic rate of customer retention, has hailed him as a Brand Ambassador for the LIC.

If the premium falls due on a policy even if he had sold it fifteen years ago, Mr Gonda will remind the client about it sufficiently in advance, keeping track if the client has changed his address in the meanwhile. And this is just one of the many ways he makes himself indispensable and keeps in regular touch with his clients at the same time.

I don't sell to friends. I sell to strangers and make them my friends.

- Minoo R Gonda

A friend of ours, who works for a newspaper, selling advertising space, confided that many times he gets business purely because of the good rapport he has generated with media houses and clients. He meets his clients regularly, takes them out for lunch once in a while, gifts them a small memento with his company logo which then stands on the client's desk, subtly making the client keep him in mind. As he says, **"If your newspaper is Number One, then the client chases you. Otherwise, you have to follow the client. This is where good rapport generates sales."**

He also added that when you prove yourself good at building a healthy rapport with clients, your boss will then give you the cream of clients and accounts to handle. In fact our friend being a relative newcomer in his newspaper, was initially not given very productive and high profile accounts to handle. But because he built a fantastic rapport and managed to get good business from even those clients who had not given so much business to his newspaper in the past, his boss gave him some very good accounts to handle, which were initially being handled by senior salespersons.

He attributes a great deal of his success in his career to the effort and attention he has paid to cultivating genuine rapport and friendship with his client base.

Another by-product of these business friendships is that on those rare occasions when you may be unable to meet your commitments for some genuine reason, your clients, if they are now your friends, would be in a better frame of mind to excuse you for your lapses.

It is similar to a minor car accident, where both drivers alight from their car in a rage to lay the blame at the door of the opposite driver, and then find out that they both know each other and are friends. The rage immediately dissolves. They may even hug each other before they go their separate ways.

We are not advocating that you become lazy in your approach with your regular clients who are your friends, but in case of genuine occasional lapses, the friendship factor would take over in your favour. And in case such lapses do occur on your part, you should take time and make efforts to make it up as soon as possible to the client in some special way. This will demonstrate your sincere concern to keep the friendship going.

The Brains Trust Pearl:
Business relationships cannot sustain for long without the vital element of friendship.

26

The 'Moment of Truth' is where all sales come from,
the 'Moment of Truth' is of importance prime

In business, the 'Moment of Truth' is all encompassing;
a great one helps you win each time

The definition of the term 'Moment-of-Truth' is a simple one.

Each time that a customer of yours encounters your brand or your brand representative, he experiences a Moment-of-Truth. Based on the customer's experience, observation and perspective, that Moment-of-Truth for him could be an unpleasant and negative one, or a pleasant and positive one.

Customers ultimately make their purchase decisions based on the Moments-of-Truth they have encountered while interacting with brands and their representatives. Customers silently perform informal, sometimes even subconscious, but highly accurate mental evaluations and calculations based on what they have seen the brand and its representatives say and do.

It is very similar to the manner in which an interviewer would be mentally evaluating the pluses and minuses of every applicant he interviews, from which he has to select the most suitable one for the post which is vacant.

The essence of the concept of Moment-of-Truth lies in the mutually beneficial outcome of Win-Win.

- Cyrus M Gonda, Dr. Kalim Khan

Just as the job interview situation would have the most suitable culmination if the organisation hired the applicant of its choice, as well as the applicant got the profile and pay package he desired (Win-Win), so too in a sales situation, Win-Win occurs when the organisation is able to make a sale at a reasonable profit, ensuring that the customer also feels satisfied that he has secured a deal which gives him good value.

Multiple and sometimes unimaginable parameters and perspectives constitute Moments-of-Truth for the customer. Different customers being individuals with different tastes and different priorities, it is but natural that their focus will lie on different attributes of their interactions with the brand.

So Step One to developing healthy Moments-of-Truth lies in understanding what aspects of the sale are of importance to each individual customer, and then proceeding to craft each customer experience accordingly.

Whatever the priorities or over-riding concerns of that individual customer, you as a salesperson need to make them your priorities as well. In the ultimate analysis, it is imperative that the customer gets the genuine feeling that the brand and the salesperson he has interacted with are 'there for him', and that they have his best interest at heart and act accordingly.

As far as safe-guarding the interest of your customer goes (to ensure that he receives a positive Moment-of-Truth from your end), **our advice for all salespersons would be that they should attempt to emulate the British bulldog, the ultimate symbol of determination and tenacity**.

We recall a civil matter that our institute was contesting. We had a choice of selecting one of two lawyers specialising in that field to represent us. Another knowledgeable lawyer, a friend of ours, advised us to put our faith in the second choice. He said, **"The first gentleman is a little more polished, slightly more well read, and relatively more articulate. But if he observes the body language of the judge is going against him, he loses his composure and literally gives up.**

The second lawyer on the other hand, is like a bloodhound. He sinks his teeth into the case. He figuratively rolls all over the floor like a dog grabbing a bone. He is tenacious, irrespective of the body language of the judge. **HIS ONLY AIM IS THAT HIS CLIENT SHOULD WIN."**

This second lawyer performs his job to the best of his ability on behalf of his customer, gaining the confidence of his client at each opportunity he gets to generate a positive Moment-of-Truth.

As someone rightly said – **You can't lose if your customer wins.**

If you as a salesperson can develop this quality and ability of tenacity, and carry it through in developing your system of working, your product knowledge, customer knowledge, competitor knowledge, and use this knowledge for the right reasons, **THIS UNDIMINISHED DRIVE** could be the **single most important quality determining your success.**

This will always lead to positive experiences and Moments-of-Truth for you as well as for your customers.

> *If you persist in supporting your customer in the right manner for the right reasons, where others in your place would have given up, you will achieve success in your sales career.*
>
> - Cyrus M Gonda, Dr. Kalim Khan

And this has to be done by you, time after time after time.

- Ask a cricketer who starts a new innings
- Or a teacher entering a new class
- Or an author commencing to work on a new book

Irrespective of their past performance, every innings, every lecture, every book, starts from scratch.

Each interaction is a fresh Moment-of-Truth.

> *Your current score is never a function of your past achievement.*
>
> - Cyrus M Gonda, Dr. Kalim Khan

A Parsee function caterer, **Joss Banquets,** has a brilliant strategy for ensuring positive Moments-of-Truth for each of his clients. He commits to undertaking only one function a day, (unlike other caterers), so personal supervision by the owner himself throughout the duration of the function is assured.

This is his key for ensuring maximum positive Moments-of-Truth. As a result, he does roaring business. Rarely does a day go by when he is not booked for a big event to cater to. And he increasingly gets orders for larger and more lucrative functions. And over time, maximum revenue generation occurs, as customers crave for his services. We asked the person at the helm of affairs at Joss Caterers the reason for his policy.

His response was, **"I want EVERY Moment-of-Truth for EACH client of mine to be a special one. My business will automatically grow."**

We are not advocating that you restrict your clientele. **What we are learning from Joss is the attitude of excellence concerning positive Moments-of-Truth.** And as a salesperson, each day you will be presented with multiple opportunities to create positive and memorable Moments-of-Truth for your prospects and for your customers.

All Moments-of-Truth ultimately need to be crafted in one direction – that of a pleasant customer experience.

- Cyrus M Gonda, Dr. Kalim Khan

The Brains Trust Pearl:
Focus on each point of your customer interaction. These points occur where the rubber hits the road.

27

Others speaking on your behalf,
will make your reputation soar

When others recommend your services,
prospects trust you more and more

Word-of-Mouth publicity is the most effective form of advertising. And what's more, it is totally free.

Reflect on the last few purchases you made which required some degree of decision making on your part. It's a safe bet that for at least some of these purchases, you consulted friends and acquaintances if they could recommend a suitable, trusted salesperson or service provider.

Let recommendations from satisfied customers become your primary marketing tool.

- Cyrus M Gonda, Dr. Kalim Khan

No film star or sports personality paid to be your brand endorser can generate even a small percentage of the credibility that a happy customer recommending your services can do.

Provide excellent service in all respects to your existing clients and customers. This will make them want to provide you with glowing testimonials. Politely and confidently request for these testimonials in writing, once you're sure that the client is thoroughly satisfied with your levels of sales and service excellence. Laminate these testimonials. It is the best way to create a positive impact on a new prospect. And this is possible to do in whichever industry you are.

Customers too would like to identify an excellent service provider and stick to him like glue. **Narrating one's own service experiences has become a leading topic of discussion at many social events, where people discuss the various brands and salespersons from whom they've received outstanding experiences.**

If individuals can become raving fans of movie stars and sportspersons who they've never personally met, simply on the strength of their powerful performances on screen and on the field, customers definitely become fans of outstanding brands and outstanding salespersons whose performances they've personally experienced and benefited from, and wholeheartedly recommend them to all their friends and acquaintances.

But just as average stars and sportspersons are soon forgotten, and only the truly outstanding ones glowingly remembered, the same holds true for salespersons.

As an exercise, attempt to identify how many of your existing clients are recommending your services to their friends and acquaintances. Please reward these well-wishers of yours in a small, intangible way, as it is their good wishes and recommendations which are responsible for making your business grow.

There is a direct co-relation between the efforts that you as a salesperson undertake to guide and service existing customers, and the positive Word-of-Mouth publicity that they in turn will churn in your favour among their vast circle of friends and relatives. We are all customers for different products and services many times every day.

And most of us actively enquire with friends and acquaintances whether they can recommend to us someone who is trustworthy, reliable and efficient in respect to a product or service that we are looking for. And if we are convinced that our friends and acquaintances have been served well, that's the salesperson we would give our business to.

At Brains Trust Training and Management Consultancy, a huge volume of our business for conducting training workshops and consultancy assignments for our corporate clientele comes through referrals from delighted participants, who spread the good word on our behalf. We rarely spend a rupee on publicising the services we offer.

This should be the aim of every one of you salespersons – To generate as much positive Word-of-Mouth publicity as possible for the goods and services that you are a provider of.

There are two reasons why any individual would become **YOUR** customer.

One reason could be that he needs the products or services which you provide. This step is essential. But it is not sufficient. If this is the only reason, then he could also avail of the same from other salespersons representing your organisation.

The second reason will ensure that the customer remains loyal to you as a salesperson. And this reason is the **exceptional service you provide in your own unique way, leaving a signature to your job that no other salesperson can or will, which endears you to the customer.** So often, when a new salesperson approaches a client who has been associated with the brand for long, the client may refuse to deal with him, saying **"Where is my regular salesperson? I feel comfortable in dealing through him."** This is the stage of relationship you should aim to reach with your customer. Not only will he remain your loyal customer for life, he will be a source of free referrals for you that could generate more business than you could possibly dream of.

The benefit for you as a salesperson of creating satisfying experiences, which will lead to positive Word-of-Mouth publicity in your favour, is that the benefit of such referrals does not merely come to the brand that you represent. The benefit comes directly to **YOU** as an individual.

So unlike advertising, which only benefits the brand as a whole, the power of positive Word-of-Mouth publicity brings personal benefits to you as an outstanding individual, representing that brand.

In fact, for us, the measure of the goodness of a salesperson is the number of new clients who have been referred to him by his delighted existing client base. (At Brains Trust, we have developed a specific training workshop on how to generate business through referrals.) Unfortunately, most organisations do not take this referral factor as a parameter of the productivity of a salesperson, while we at Brains Trust Management Consultancy very strongly include this as a measure for the success of a salesperson when we provide consultancy services to organisations for assessing the effectiveness of their salespersons.

A few questions for you as a salesperson. In your role as a customer:

- Have you not recommended restaurants with excellent food and service to your friends?
- Have you not recommended excellent movies and books?
- Have you not recommended a good brand of television or washing machine, and a good sales outlet to purchase it from?
- Have you not recommended a good vacation resort?

Now let's go a step further. In all the above recommendations you may have made, there would be certain commonalities:

- The element of quality
- The factor of convenience
- The trust factor through the faith you have in that product or service provider based on every past experience with him being a positive one
- And most important of all, no one would have forced you to provide the recommendation. You did it willingly

So what are some of the **advantages for you** when your customers recommend you to their friends, colleagues, relatives and others who fall under their sphere of influence?

- You are sure that your existing customers are happy with you
- Your customer base widens
- Your revenue generation increases
- You have less need to conduct cold calls

We rest our case.

The Brains Trust Pearl:
Generate positive Word-of-Mouth publicity and referrals for yourself, by actions that make you Top-of-the-Mind recall in your product category for your customer.

28

Joining, mixing, merging, mingling;
will help you generate revenue

Network, network, always network;
business opportunities will improve

In the corporate world today, having a network of individuals who know you and like you and who appreciate your professional approach is an essential tool for achieving sales success.

It is your task as a salesperson to actively enhance this network at every opportunity you get. It takes systematic effort on your part to enhance and maintain this network, but the returns you get will be spectacular.

Networking is a skill that successful salespersons take great pains to develop.

Many organisations are now conducting interviews to recruit new salespersons not in their own office premises, but in a restaurant, or in the food-court of a mall; over breakfast or lunch or dinner. The logic is clear. Today, a majority of business deals are struck in an informal environment at neutral venues such as a club or a food outlet. Organisations want to assure themselves that the salesperson they recruit would be comfortable conducting business in such an environment.

And it is not only the environment in which business occurs that has changed. **Clients today prefer to deal with salespersons with whom they can carry on intelligent conversations on topics of general interest.**

The rule to be followed during business dinners is – Business must not be discussed till the coffee after the meal is being served.

Does that mean that the salesperson must keep quiet throughout dinner? Not at all. He is expected to chat, to converse, to interact on:

- The latest movies and books
- Happenings in sports
- Domestic and International politics
- Developments in science

and any other topic under the sun that takes the client's fancy.

So a salesperson must always be well read, well informed and articulate in areas of general knowledge and current affairs.

The more topics he is familiar and comfortable with, the greater will be his confidence level to interact with clients in an informal environment.

We remember at a recent business dinner we were part of, the topic of the **origin of different calendars of the world** casually came up.

From there, the discussion moved on to:

- The Hindu calendar
- The Islamic calendar
- The Christian calendar
- The similarities and the differences among them
- The specific need of the various people they served

From there the talk moved on to related areas such as:

- Mythology
- Folklore
- Astronomy
- Astrology

It was a fascinating discussion, and the meal stretched for over two hours.

Every individual at the table was well informed and well read in each of these areas, (which apparently have nothing to do with business), and each individual contributed some interesting insights and tit-bits to the animated discussion. Needless to say, everyone left the dinner table feeling much more cordial and closer to each other. The business deal was then a foregone conclusion.

A single conversation across the table with a wise man is better than ten years mere study of books.

- Henry Wadsworth Longfellow

Some friends of ours were down from the USA recently, and since they were in senior positions in sales and business development there, we naturally asked them about the current trends in the field of sales in their home country.

The gist of their input was – Today, if you are in the sales profession, and are excellent at your work, but you wish to go home by six in the evening and have dinner with your family every day, then rising to a high level of hierarchy in the sales function would be very difficult.

The reason for this is, most business today happens **AFTER** office hours, and individuals in the field of selling need to network and socialise, and enjoy it. **As a salesperson, you should make the most of any networking and socialising opportunity that comes your way.**

Poverty, I realised, wasn't only a lack of financial resources; it was isolation from the kind of people that could help you make more of yourself.

- Keith Ferrazzi

We were once scheduled to give a brief talk on the subject of leadership at a prestigious club. It was an appreciative audience, comprising of entrepreneurs and businesspersons. While our talk was underway, the organisers got a message that the person (a member of their club), who was supposed to deliver the felicitation speech after our talk, was not going to turn up. He was the person who regularly gave this thank-you speech at all their functions. The club relied on him for this task. No other club member present was comfortable with the idea of standing up in front of the audience and delivering an impromptu felicitation speech.

The cameraman who was hired by the club to photo-shoot the event overheard the committee members of the club discussing their problem. Being an outgoing and helpful person by nature, he proactively volunteered to do the job for them. The organisers gratefully accepted his offer, and the man did a brilliant job.

This brought him in the public eye of the members of that club, and he began informally interacting with them once the function was over. He developed this rapport, and soon became a part of the social group himself. We also, are still in touch with this gentleman.

Today, a year later, he says that literally thirty percent of his current business comes through the members of the club who were present on the day he offered to give the felicitation speech.

Strangers are just friends who haven't yet met.

- Peter Rosen

There is a group of individuals from different fields of business who religiously meet up once a week for the express purpose of business networking. Various chapters of this networking group exist in different geographical locations. The condition for membership being, that in each group, not more than one individual or organisation from any one industry will be admitted and represented, so as to ensure there is no internal competition among members of that group. For example, in one group you would find a person representing:

- An insurance company
- A corporate trainer in the field of soft skills
- A caterer
- A travel agent
- A website developer

and many, many more.

The objective of this weekly meeting is to keep in touch with other members and tell them the latest happenings and offerings in your business, so they can promote your products and services to all people whom they know and who would be interested in the same.

Each member promotes the business of every other member.

Thus, every member automatically has around twenty dedicated salespersons working on his behalf, free of cost. Many members of the group say that a huge chunk of their sales comes through this regular networking exercise, which lasts for just a couple of hours each week. Nothing prevents you from profitably joining, or even initiating similar groups of your own.

A point to keep in mind about networking.

Like every other activity, the benefits of networking will bear full fruit if the process of networking is conducted by you in a **systematic** and **organised**, rather than in a haphazard manner.

Maintain and constantly update a well-structured database of contacts you have developed, writing references as to where and through whom you have met them, and what do they do. This will help you when you go through your list of contacts at festival time, helping you to know which contact should be wished on which occasion, and how long it has been since you last kept in touch. Just a simple 'Hello' works wonders to strengthen a relationship.

A structured and regularly updated database of contacts you have met personally and professionally, is a fantastic tool which will help you further your sales career, merely by using it intelligently. Use this tool wisely and use it well.

Call it a clan, call it a network, call it a tribe, call it a family. Whatever you call it, whoever you are, you need one.

- Jane Howard

The Brains Trust Pearl:

Invest time and effort in building a professional and personal network of acquaintances which will rival a spider's web. The positive returns of such a network for your business are simply unimaginable.

29

Price comes later, price comes after,
price is always secondary

First show value, genuine value,
of what use you can be to me

This is your customer speaking.

And he's telling you very clearly, that value matters to him more than price does.

The terms **price** and **value** do not mean the same thing. They differ. Vastly.

As a salesperson, you need to understand the critical difference between the terms **price** and **value**.

Price refers to what is displayed on the price tag.

It is a **tangible** element.

Value rests in the mind of the customer.

It is apparently **intangible.**

Yet value matters. It matters a lot.

One fact that the experts in the field of management agree upon, is that today, **the intangible element in business transactions matters more than the tangible.**

Sensible salespersons focus on value, not on price.

If the product or service you are offering does not hold value for the prospect, even at the lowest price that you can afford to offer it, the customer will not be induced to buy.

And the moment you as a salesperson start speaking the language of low price and discounts, the customer will seize the opportunity, and ask for further discounts.

We were recently discussing the purchase of some pieces of capital equipment for our institute with a vendor who had sought an appointment to present his brand. Right from the start of his presentation, the vendor kept saying – "You tell us the volumes you require and we will tell you the discount we can offer." We ended the presentation there itself. Of course price is an important element of any purchase decision, but not in this manner. Such a salesperson demeans the brand he represents.

What he is saying in effect is – **"My product is so bad, it will not sell unless I provide the lure of a discount."**

Discounts and freebies are to be used sparingly and rationally. Not to be used at Step One or even at Step Two of your presentation. Priority in your presentation should be given to the value addition that your brand of product or service can provide the prospect.

Here we would like to elaborate on an area we briefly touched upon in a previous couplet. This area being the comparison between the two terms – **Features** and **Benefits**.

A typical mistake committed by many salespersons is that throughout their sales presentation, they focus on the features of their product or service, and sometimes on the advantages. But rarely have we come across these features and advantages categorically being communicated in the form of benefits.

Let us get one thing very clear, that any purchase anywhere, of any product or service, is always done by the customer, keeping an end benefit in mind. Features and advantages alone can never, ever be the reason for a purchase decision.

We have very often heard salespersons during presentations make statements such as:

- It is made of steel
- It has the highest TRP
- It contains PSPO
- It has the highest resolutions

and so on. All these sentences would inevitably have the customer consciously or sub-consciously asking – **So what'**?

As we all know, no customer ever purchases a drill machine. He is purchasing a hole in the wall.

Also while on this topic, keep in mind not to spend valuable presentation time informing the prospect about the glorious past of your company. Your customer is more interested in knowing what your products and services can do for him today. The following superb piece of poetry (author unfortunately unknown), brings out this point in brilliant fashion.

AN ODE TO BENEFITS

I see that you've spent quite a big wad of dough
To tell me the things you think I should know.
How your plant is so big, so fine, so strong;
And your founder has whiskers so handsomely long.
So he started the business way back in 1892?
How tremendously interesting this is – to YOU.
He built up the brand with the blood of his life?
I'll run home right now and tell that to my wife.
Your machinery's modern and, oh, so complete!
Your rep is so flawless, your workers so neat.
Your motto is "Quality" – capital "Q".
No wonder I'm getting tired of "your" and of "you".
So tell me quick and tell me true.
(Or else, my friend, to heck with you!)
LESS: How this product came to be.
MORE: What the darn thing DOES FOR ME!

- Unknown

A good salesperson would ensure that his company history, and the features and advantages of his product or service are enumerated, explained and demonstrated only to explicitly bring out the benefits that can be accrued to the customer. They serve no other purpose.

Never, ever, in your entire sales career, forget this one truth. For once the benefits of your product or service are clearly enumerated and these match the customer's needs, value will be determined, and then the issue of price will be of secondary importance as compared to the value received.

We are aware of an accounts coaching class run by an accountancy genius, who charges the highest rates among all such classes. Yet the maximum number of students rush there to secure admission as this professor provides immense value for the high fees he charges. The results of his students speak for themselves.

There are many potential customers willing to pay the price you ask for. The question is, are you able to deliver the value they seek?

- Cyrus M Gonda, Dr. Kalim Khan

Xtreme Personal Assistant and Concierge Services is the organisation that the rich and famous of the world approach to pamper their desires.

When a certain celebrity requested **Scott Graham**, the **CEO** of **'Xtreme'** to deliver a steaming hot, fresh pepperoni pizza to his flat in **London, England,** it didn't seem such an odd request. But there was a catch. (There always is a catch, isn't there?). The celebrity wanted the pizza to come from a particular restaurant in **Chicago, USA**. The customer was testing Scott's ability to deliver, and Scott delivered in style.

The **motto of 'Xtreme'** is **"Anything and everything, as long as it's moral, ethical and legal."**

As 'Xtreme' puts it, **"If you can imagine it, we can deliver it."**

The 'Xtreme' team loaded a private plane with a chef and a pizza oven.

They picked up the prepared but uncooked pizza in Chicago and it was put in the oven to bake just as the plane was landing in London. A vehicle waiting at London airport rushed the steaming pizza to the delighted customer just at the time he had requested for it.

Scott earned a neat profit on the transaction, along with a lot of referral business from the delighted celebrity.

The delighted client told Scott – **"You have a customer for life."**

There is an increasingly growing volume of clientele for whom price is not as much an issue as is the value that the service provider can deliver.

- Cyrus M Gonda, Dr. Kalim Khan

The Brains Trust Pearl:
Demonstrate the overall value that your unique product and service can provide to the customer. Then price will not be an unbreakable barrier.

30

Can your customers do without you?
Don't be mistaken; yes they can

No one on earth is indispensable,
but strive to be your customer's right hand man

Presidents, kings, emperors, have passed on, and the world still moves ahead at its own steady pace.

Make no mistake. No one is indispensable. And even if someone truly is indispensable, it is best for him to think that he is not, and never can be. Else the unfortunate element of arrogance steadily creeps into one's own attitude and behaviour.

So the seemingly contradictory message here is – **Do your best to truly become indispensable as a sales and service provider to your customers, but simultaneously refrain from thinking and feeling that you are indispensable.**

No one on Planet Earth is indispensable.

Often we have heard this.

But deep down, many of us mistakenly feel that this does not apply to us as individuals.

If you possess this attitude, eliminate it as soon as possible.

There are some organisations, currently operating in a monopoly-like situation, which begin to function like rationing officers. They start to think that their customers cannot do without them. And this thought process is bound to lead to arrogance. It is a law of nature.

The path to sales success is to ensure that this attitude, if currently present, moves out of your life forever.

The ideal situation from the customer's perspective would be if you did provide that level of excellence and efficiency which would make you indispensable, without you developing the attitude that you are indispensable. This is a sure fire recipe for sales success.

If only I had a little humility, I'd be perfect.

- Ted Turner

In today's fast paced world, where technology and new products can be duplicated by competitors in a short span of time, it is extremely difficult for a brand to possess a product differentiation or a product USP.

The only differentiators among competing organisations today are the Service USPs, which you as a Super Salesperson have it within your power to generate.

In order to achieve true indispensability in your actions, (not just in your thoughts), you need to identify all the thousand and one extras that you as a Super Salesperson could do to keep yourself firmly and positively entrenched in the mind of your customers.

You may be surprised to discover that most of these thousand and one ways cost you no money at all, but would require you to devote your time and your genuine care, apply your mind intelligently and put in your honest effort.

This is where the **Japanese concept** of **Kaizen,** or **Continuous Improvement**, is extremely relevant for a Super Salesperson. **He should learn 'something' worthwhile, however minor it may seem, from each customer interaction.** That 'something' which is learned needs to be kept in mind for all future customer interactions. If that 'something' was an error, it needs to be minimised, and ultimately eliminated. If that 'something' was a good gesture which was appreciated by the customer, it needs to be repeated by you till it becomes a habit.

Continuous improvement is the key to success in selling.

- Cyrus M Gonda, Dr. Kalim Khan

No better example of indispensability and being outstandingly and positively different from other salespersons can be provided than that of a Super Salesperson we are honoured to know. He has today reached the pinnacle in the publishing industry.

He is a gentleman by the name of **Naval Shukla**. We had the privilege of being his customers when he used to market text books and other publications to management institutes in the city of Mumbai. At that time, he represented a particular publishing house. There were many other salespersons that represented other publishing houses who also interacted with the faculty of management institutes.

All of these salespersons were good people. But among them all, Naval Shukla was outstanding. Even compared with other salespersons from his own organisation, Naval stood out miles ahead.

Ironically, Naval never openly made attempts to sell his books, yet all the books he displayed got sold out.

Let us examine, analyse, understand and attempt to replicate the unique approach that Naval adopted.

In the first place, however friendly and close he got with his customers, he maintained his level of professionalism. Even after he became friends with his customers, he never dropped in without prior appointment. He never ever took his customers for granted. This is something which his customers appreciated.

He also made substantial efforts to learn and understand the core interest and subject area of every faculty member he interacted with. He then made a note of that area.

On a regular basis, he would send across an interesting snippet, specific to the subject area and area of interest of individual faculties, just letting them know that he thought this might be of interest to them.

Faculty eagerly awaited these snippets, which were always welcomed for the knowledge and information they contained. The faculty's relationship with Naval strengthened.

All this did not happen without a lot of hard and smart work combined with initiative on Naval's part. He invested a lot of his time in conducting relevant research, which made his snippets and relevant quotations so appropriate and special for the individual faculty he interacted with. He researched sites which would be of interest to the individual faculty and sent across links to these sites.

In his own quiet way, Naval became indispensable to his customers, not for the books he displayed to sell, but for the quality of becoming a true right hand man.

Unlike other book salespersons that visited and interacted with faculty just once a year, which was only at the time when they wanted to make a sale, Naval on the other hand was always top-of-mind.

And he did this without disturbing the work time of the customers. In fact, let alone being a disturbance or interference, he was a welcome value addition to the work process of his customers.

He used to advise faculty on good books they could make use of, even though these books may not have been from his publishing house, and he would be generating no immediate sales for himself by recommending them. The dividends that these actions paid him led him to become the indispensable and trusted advisor that faculty members were looking for.

In short, he soon established himself as a trusted expert and a one point contact for faculty for management publications.

His was the only name among book salespersons that faculty would remember.

This approach is possible to use for salespersons in any industry, not only for publishing house representatives. Learn to identify the area of professional interest as well as the hobby of your customers. Research it. Collect regular information on it. Send it across to your customer as a gentle reminder of your indispensability.

Identify the other thousand and one things you as a Super Salesperson can do. Become truly indispensable without thinking that you are indispensable, and start off on the path to sales success.

*It was pride that changed angels into devils; it is humility
that makes men as angels.*

- Saint Augustine

It is only the highest level of professional competency that can
create indispensability.

As an example, the amount of effort that **Lata Mangeshkar** has
put into developing her voice resulted into many leading female
actresses saying they would act in a movie only if Lata sang their
songs for them. **For these leading actresses, no other playback
singer would do**.

Or the classic example of the **Number Ten Tee-Shirt in a soccer
team** being reserved for the most indispensable player in the team.

At **Brains Trust Management Consultancy**, we have developed
a formula which you can use to measure how indispensable you are
as a salesperson, or how indispensable the salespersons in your
organisation are to your customers.

Brains Trust Formula for Salesperson Indispensability

*Magnitude of Salesperson Indispensability = Competency
of the Salesperson X Attitude to Serve*

Both the parameters of Competency as well as Attitude need to be
rated on a scale of 0 to 10.

This formula can be used by organisations to evaluate their sales
force, as well as by proactive salespersons who wish to honestly and
constantly evolve and improve themselves on the vital parameter
of Customer Indispensability.

For organisations that wish to evaluate their salespersons, we at
Brains Trust Management Consultancy have developed metrics to
measure Magnitude of Customer Indispensability on certain
parameters.

Be faithful to that which exists nowhere but in yourself – and thus make yourself indispensable.

- Andre Gide

The Brains Trust Pearl:
If you can become truly indispensable without feeling proud about it, success as a salesperson is yours for the asking.

31

**Giving feedback to the management
is part of every salesperson's task**

**Feedback from your customers,
it is your job to ask**

The process of open, transparent and two-way communication is at the core and heart of all healthy relationships.

This also holds true for the three pronged relationship that exists among the salesperson, his organisation on one hand, and his customer on the other.

The process of communication remains incomplete until the vital element of feedback is actively sought and acted upon.

- Cyrus M Gonda, Dr. Kalim Khan

In the relationship between the salesperson and his customer, it is the active soliciting of feedback by the salesperson which transforms the relationship onto a higher platform.

Feedback from a customer to a salesperson is very much like the feedback provided by a **coach to a sportsperson.**

Both the coach, as well as the customer, are in the best possible position to observe shortcomings and possible areas of improvement.

We have observed in many instances, that it is customers who provide wonderful and practical feedback to the salespersons they interact with. This feedback could be with regard to some element of product or service quality, an additional feature they would like to see introduced, or they may simply be expressing their opinions, likes, dislikes, tastes and preferences about the product or service.

These insights come absolutely free of cost, and they come from the person who matters the most – **Your Customer**.

Yet in most cases, these valuable insights and feedback tend to go into one ear and out of the other. This is such a pity.

The management should actively solicit and anxiously await such feedback through salespersons as it can be the key to better decision making with regards to product and service innovation, delivery and payment policies and also in other areas, which could better satisfy the customer.

If this feedback from the customer was dutifully passed on to the management, all three parties concerned would greatly benefit.

The three parties being – The management, the customer, and most important of all, the salesperson himself.

The **management benefits** by implementing this feedback which originated from the customer as it would lead to enhanced revenue, cost reduction, system and process enhancement, customer delight and first mover advantage. This would ultimately lead to higher market share, profitability and a stronger brand. After all, the more a brand satisfies the needs and expectations of its customers, the stronger the brand becomes.

The **customer benefits**, as some of the sensible suggestions he provides get incorporated into the product or service and he gets the benefit of using an enhanced product or service, which is more to his taste and liking. He also gets the psychological boost of knowing that the salesperson he deals with and the brand to which he is a customer, care sufficiently about him to ask him for his inputs and suggestions and also implement those suggestions which are feasible.

The **salesperson benefits the maximum.** A salesperson who performs this task of gathering customer feedback and passes it on to the management, elevates himself to a higher level. He is considered suitable for handling managerial responsibilities. It gives his career a boost and may get him financial rewards in the form of incentives if the suggestions he passes on are well received. It would also improve his rapport and relationship with his customers and bring him closer to them.

Feedback provided by the salesperson could also be in the form of customer complaints and negative comments from aggrieved customers. In fact, this type of feedback should be given top priority, as if such type of feedback is acted upon speedily and grievances are rectified, a customer who otherwise could have been lost to the brand forever could be happily retained.

So you, the salesperson, are the vital link in the chain between your Organisation – its products, services and policies on one hand; and the Customer – his needs, his requirements and his preferences on the other.

> *You as a salesperson are the eyes and ears of your organisation.*
>
> - Cyrus M Gonda, Dr. Kalim Khan

Product innovation, service streamlining and enhancement of policies to suit your customers will all happen once you play this role to perfection. No one is in a better position than you are as far as this vital task is concerned. In many instances, salespersons get tremendous inputs from customers but they never pass it on to their management.

Salespersons who practice the act of soliciting and passing on feedback from customers no longer remain mere salespersons. In the eyes of their customers and their management, **such salespersons then acquire the reputation of a valued consultant, a professional.**

It is surprising that in all other business situations, feedback is actively undertaken. When an advertisement is aired, the management sets in motion a mechanism of feedback to test its effectiveness. The same is true when a new product or service is launched or some new business initiative is undertaken.

Similarly, in the key area of interaction between the customer and salesperson, feedback needs to be considered as an active parameter of review, else the process of sales loses most of its meaning.

We are aware of an organisation which designs and manufactures modular furniture for corporate use. A particular salesperson from this organisation was dealing with a key-account where he got involved with the furnishing of their new branch.

This experience and the inputs that he received regarding the design of the furniture from this client in the process of selling to them were passed on as feedback to his own design team, which then incorporated many of the client's suggestions in future designs.

These inputs were highly practical and once they were incorporated, they were appreciated by other clients as well. In fact, based on this detailed and substantial feedback, a whole new line of office furniture was developed, and the salesperson who had initially provided this feedback was put in charge of this new division.

We believe that feedback is the only mechanism that can bring about continuous improvements in an organisation's existing process, products and services.

It is rightly said – **Feedback is the breakfast of champions.**

The Brains Trust Pearl:
Paying attention to the vital function of customer feedback transforms you from the level of a salesperson to the level of a consultant. Your career zooms on to the fast track.

32

If you follow all our simple rules
ten times out of ten

Then we're sure you will never face
real problems ever again

Read this last couplet of the Super Salesperson's Song carefully.

Very, very carefully.

It says that all the qualities, attributes and habits we have mentioned throughout the 'Song of the Super Salesperson' are **interlinked** with one another.

It is just not possible to succeed in your sales career by focusing on developing those qualities or habits which you feel are convenient to follow or which suit you, and ignoring the rest.

> *It is not as though your customer would pardon you for a delayed response to his query, simply because you have managed to remember his birthday.*

> - Cyrus M Gonda, Dr. Kalim Khan

No. Selling doesn't work that way.

Neither does any other relationship in your life.

We have formulated all these qualities, attributes and habits put together to devise the Comprehensive Success Model laid out in this book for a Super Salesperson to follow. All of them put together will definitely assure success.

These thirty two qualities, attributes and habits are the result of a decade of work at our end in researching, interviewing and following the careers of top performing salespersons across industry.

(For the record, **the two of us authors** have been acknowledged as **India's leading experts on Customer Service** by **Murali Gopalan,** the **Business Editor of The Hindu Business Line,** which is a highly respected source of business information in India.)

Attaining mastery in only a few of these thirty two qualities will not serve your purpose.

There is no sense in going to a gymnasium with the objective of developing your physique, and then focusing on exercising only your arms, or your chest, or your legs, or any one body part. The result of such activity will be a skewed, lopsided mockery of a human body.

\- Cyrus M Gonda, Dr. Kalim Khan

In **Indian philosophy,** we have the science of:

- **Hatha Yoga** - To be followed for strengthening the physical body
- **Raja Yoga** - For developing will power and mental faculties
- **Gnani Yoga** - For studying the fundamental principles and truths underlying life
- **Bhakti Yoga** - For joining in union with the One through the influence of love

A rounded knowledge of each of the above four sciences is considered essential to attain salvation.

Mastery in only one or two of these four branches serves little purpose.

With this book, we give a money back guarantee that if the qualities, traits and habits which we have enumerated are developed and repeatedly practiced by you over a period of time, you **WILL** transform yourself into a Super Salesperson. It is our guarantee.

But you need to practice **ALL** the attributes and develop **ALL** the habits we have mentioned to attain success.

It is not at all difficult.

Approach the task methodically. Step by step.

A holistic approach is absolutely essential.

Setting time periods for yourself to strengthen in the areas which you feel you need to develop.

The thirty two attributes enumerated in this book have been identified by us through years of study and observation. We have benchmarked these attributes from the most successful salespersons the world has ever seen.

If any single attribute is missing in your toolbox, the final output would be negatively affected.

Individual attributes are like individual pearls; by themselves valuable, but when strung together to complete a beautiful necklace, they become priceless.

- Cyrus M Gonda, Dr. Kalim Khan

If any one of these attributes, qualities or habits is missing in your approach towards your customers – **It is like an important letter of the alphabet missing on the keyboard.**

It is very like a student securing cent percent marks in five subjects, and failing by just one mark in the sixth subject. This student would be awarded five gold medals for attaining mastery in five individual subjects.

But his overall result would be a failure.

All because he ignored one vital area essential for overall success.

When we say that attaining mastery in all the attributes we have identified will ensure that you as a salesperson never face real problems again, we would like to elaborate on the same.

For any salesperson, the **REAL PROBLEMS** he could face are loss of faith, trust and credibility in the eyes of the customer.

A real problem that a salesperson could face is having a door slammed in his face because his negative reputation precedes him.

Any other problems that you as a salesperson could face are merely temporary.

They would be minor setbacks which can be systematically overcome with the right training and effort. These other minor problems would actually be stepping stones along the path to success, because if the right attributes and habits have been developed, you are already on the right path.

These temporary 'other' problems can never be classified as real or genuine problems.

But the burden of the problems that come with loss of credibility will be more than you or your career can ever bear.

You must understand the whole of life, not just one little part of it. That is why you must read, that is why you must look at the skies, that is why you must sing, and dance, and write poems, and suffer, and understand, for all that is life.

- Unknown

The Brains Trust Pearl:

Crafting a successful sales career is about creating for yourself a blend of positive attributes and habits, in the same way that different instruments pleasingly merge to form a beautiful symphony. Goodness in a single or even in a few attributes can never ever get you sales success. It is the harmony and integration of all necessary attributes in the right combination which ensures sales victory.

CHECKLISTS

Checklist #1

Personal Upkeep

- Well ironed and spotless clothing
- No frayed shirt collars
- No frayed sleeve cuffs on shirt
- If white shirt, take extra care. Stains immediately show up
- If dark shirt, take care. Dandruff shows up
- Do not wear the same shirt two days in a row
- If possible, keep a spare shirt in office
- Shirt sleeves never to be rolled up
- Only extreme top button on shirt to be left undone in case you are not sporting a tie
- Avoid heavy designs, heavy stripes, and dark or fluorescent colours on shirt
- In case, you are sporting a tie, it should match your overall attire
- No floral designs on tie
- Jeans, corduroys and chinos are not considered formal trousers
- Gents to avoid ornaments. Ear studs and wrist bracelets are best avoided
- Hair to be neatly and regularly trimmed. Avoid fancy hairstyles
- Avoid going for client meets with excessive hair oil applied
- Be clean shaven every day. If sporting a beard, ensure it is regularly trimmed

- Gents and ladies to have well trimmed nails
- Ladies to have hair neatly set
- Ladies to have minimum of make-up and jewelry
- Ladies, if wearing nail polish, ensure it is evenly applied
- Wear a decent slim watch. Not flashy or sporty
- Gents to wear simple, neat belt with no fancy buckles or designs
- Colour of the belt should match the colour of your shoes
- Ladies should avoid shoes with high heels
- Ensure your shoes are comfortable to walk in
- Shoes should be well polished daily
- Alternate your shoes. They need a day to breathe. Will not smell and will last longer
- Socks with good elastic rolled up on calf
- Socks to be long enough to ensure that no skin shows between socks and bottom of trouser leg, even while seated
- Avoid white or light colored socks. These are not considered formal wear
- Ensure that socks are not even slightly torn as at some places you may have to remove your shoes

Checklist #2

Personal Kit

- Carry sufficient visiting cards in your card holder
- Ensure you are carrying your company identity card with you at all times
- Carry neatly stacked company information, brochures, documentation forms, invoice book, other necessary material
- Carry copies of testimonials from satisfied clients
- Carry two pens in working condition. Ensure the brands of pens are decent. Need not be expensive, but metal bodied pens are preferred.
- Gents to carry pens in top pocket of shirt
- Ladies to have pens handy in their purse
- Your bag should carry a notepad, pencils, headache pills and a packet of tissues
- Carry and use a deodorant when necessary
- Carry and use mints or mouth fresheners before a client meet
- Carry a clean handkerchief
- Carry a comb or hairbrush
- Carry an energy bar in case you have no time for lunch
- Keep sufficient change money with you for paying taxi fare and for other contingencies

- Carry sufficient cash or functional credit-card for payment of restaurant bills, in case taking a client to lunch
- Carry a small bottle of liquid stain remover in case your shirt or trousers get stained during the day

Checklist #3

Product/Service Knowledge

- Be aware of complete range in your product and service category such as models, sizes, colours, schemes and so on
- Be aware of all features of all models of products and all types of services you sell
- Be aware how features of competitor's products and services compare with your own
- Be aware of advantages of all models of products and all types of services you sell
- Be aware of benefits of all models of products and all types of services you sell
- Identify USPs of all models of products and all types of services you sell
- Be aware of current availability of stock of various models, styles, designs, colour, size and so on
- Keep track to see if new products or services introduced and familiarise yourself with features of the same
- Keep track to see if existing products or services are discontinued
- Be aware of your organisational policies regarding discounts, credit extended, payment terms, delivery schedule, and the flexibility possible in each of these
- Identify what customisation is possible in your products and services. What is the cost attached to the same
- Keep yourself updated with latest innovations in your products, your organisation and your industry

- Be conversant with demonstration of all features in your entire range of products

- Be aware of details of after-sales-terms and customer care procedure

- Be aware of details of exchange and replacement policy

- Be aware of customer grievance handling procedure

- Be conversant with the clauses in your guarantee, warranty and all fine print in documentation

- Identify hierarchy levels in your own organisation which can take specific decisions regarding discounts, replacement and so on

Checklist #4

Knowledge of Employing Organisation

- History of organisation
- Details of top management
- Various brands owned by the organisation
- Details of conglomerate, if any (Parent and Group companies)
- Geographical spread and locations
- Turnover
- Past performance
- All possible quantitative information like market share, current market price of share and so on
- Number of employees
- Awards and certifications received
- Vision and Mission Statements
- Quality Policy
- Upcoming projects
- List of current clients and key-accounts
- Credentials and testimonials from satisfied clients
- Any tie-ups your organisation has with other organisations for specific purposes which could benefit customers
- Related services or other services your parent organisation could offer

Checklist #5

Know your Customer

a) About Client Organisation

- Visit website of client organisation
- Refer websites and magazines pertaining to your client's area of business
- History of client organisation
- Full form of name of client organisation name (for example–What does ABC Ltd stand for?)
- Core and ancillary business of client organisation
- Details of conglomerate, if any (Parent company or Group companies)
- Brands that client organisation owns
- Geographical spread and locations
- Details of top management
- Turnover
- All possible quantitative information about client organisation such as market share, market price of share and so on
- Number of employees
- Awards and certifications received
- Upcoming projects
- List of key clients and customers
- Business details of client organisation
- Identify USP of your product or service from client's perspective

- Who are client's competitors
- Current happenings in client's industry
- Who else is currently serving client's need in your area of product or service
- Potential volume of business for you through this client
- Tie-ups your client organisation has with other organisations for specific purposes
- Identify whether this client organisation has dealt with your organisation in the past. Details of past interaction. Any issues pending which need to be settled to client's satisfaction, if so go prepared with solutions
- Identify key decision makers in client organisation

b) **About Key Individuals in Client Organisation**

- Key contacts in client organisation
- Name of the secretary or immediate colleague of key contact in client organisation
- Perform Google search on key individuals
- Likes, dislikes, hobbies, areas of interest of these key individuals
- Personal history and details of key individuals such as birthday, spouse name, number of children and so on
- Religious occasions that these key individuals observe
- Career details of key individuals
- Any professional, social organisations that key individuals belong to

Checklist #6

General Awareness

- Be up-to-date with latest news and current affairs
- Keep in touch with overall market happenings
- Update on happenings in your industry or sector
- National and international political updates and business impact of the same
- Keep updated with competitor activities
- Keep updated with cultural and sporting happenings–national and international
- Be up-to-date with general global trends in business and economy.
- Be aware of impact of global trends on your product and industry
- To attain awareness in above areas, read at least one general newspaper each day and one business magazine each week

Checklist #7

Personal Efficiency

- Do not carry laptop in backpacks or plastic bags. A neat briefcase is the order of the day

- Create and maintain separate physical plastic folders pertaining to paper-work of each client

- Create separate folders in your laptop for each client containing:
  1. PPT for that client
  2. Client organisation information
  3. Key individual information in that client organisation
  4. Sequential date-wise correspondence with this client
  5. A notepad containing all happenings and discussions with this client
  6. A notepad with tasks and reminders to be undertaken for this client
  7. An Excel sheet containing all relevant contact details for this client organisation

- Thoroughly check for spelling errors in client's name, company name, also for his exact designation and other details in all documents to be submitted to the client

- Always confirm and locate physical address of client organisation with landmarks before first meeting with any client

- Make it a habit to reach any meeting fifteen minutes beforehand. So schedule your meetings for the day accordingly

- It is important that your clothes and shoes feel comfortable

- At client location, use the restroom, splash water on your face, use your deodorant, have a mouth freshener, check if your shoe-laces are tied, comb your hair and check for overall appearance. Gents should never wet their hair and ladies should avoid extra last minute make-up

- Ladies to strictly avoid extra clutter in hand-bag

- Gents to ensure shirt pocket free of clutter and not bulging with notes or papers

- Avoid carrying keys and coins in your trouser pocket. These should be carried in a pouch in your carry bag

- When you receive someone's visiting card, carefully keep it in a place separate from where you keep your own. Else they may get mixed up, and you could be handing over someone else's card

- Keep a visiting card case in office or at home, and keep cards you have received in that, sorted by industry or any system convenient to you

- Avoid carrying an overstuffed and untidy wallet

- Fully charge your mobile and laptop every night

- Iron and layout your clothes and polish your shoes at night. Also pack briefcase at night, and check if all items to be carried are there

Checklist #8

Before Sales Call

- Be well versed with client organisation and details of person you will be meeting
- If possible, identify and be well versed with client requirements
- Have answers to possible client FAQs ready
- Ensure you carry all relevant documents needed for the meeting; specifically things such as quotations, testimonials and any other information the client has requested or may need
- Keep a schedule of your future appointments ready so you can immediately respond to client for scheduling next meeting
- Reach early for sales call and read company in-house magazine, journal and literature kept at reception desk
- Observe awards, certifications and trophies at client reception area
- Any queries that client has made at time of giving you an appointment, make sure you have those answers ready
- Confirm appointment of meeting through an SMS
- Check for current availability, non-availability of all models of your product prior to client meeting
- Be very sure of all specifications, features and functioning of your products. In short, detailed, in depth knowledge of all your products and services
- Have a few interesting stories ready regarding satisfied clients of your product or service

- Do not memorise your presentation, but be thorough with it

- Ensure if you are using a laptop for presentation, that it is sufficiently charged. As far as possible, avoid requesting for electrical connectivity at client location

Checklist #9

During Sales Call

- Politely knock cabin door before entering
- Give a cheerful greeting
- Maintain eye contact
- Have a genuine, pleasing smile on your face
- Wait to be told to be seated
- Store client's visiting card carefully and respectfully
- During entire presentation, do not badmouth anybody, any organisation or anything
- Do not intervene when client is talking
- Take notes of any instructions client gives
- Respect client's desk space; do not lay out your presentation material on it without his permission
- Do not make any commitments to the client that you are not confident of delivering
- Be politically neutral in your general conversation
- Indulge in conversation on current topics, movies, sports, if client initiates discussion
- Keep mobile off or on silent. Do not take calls during client meet, however big or small the meeting may be

Checklist #10

Post Sales Call

- If you have met the client for the first time, immediately store his mobile number and e-mail in your database

- If your laptop has internet connectivity, immediately send a thank you mail to the client for the opportunity for the meeting. Enumerate discussion of the meeting and further activities to be undertaken in relation thereof

- In case you do not have laptop with internet connectivity, a message would do

- Once meeting is over, immediately make a detailed list of any action to be taken from your end and any commitments you have promised the client during the meeting

- Report back with details of the meeting to your immediate boss

- Plan any follow-up action based on this meeting and implement it as soon as possible

- Send the client relevant, intermittent emails to keep him aware of status of activity

Checklist #11

Etiquette

- Avoid using slang and short-forms in your email and SMSes

- In case you smoke, strictly avoid the same before a client meet

- In case of an unavoidable delay in reaching client location for a scheduled meeting, inform the client about your delayed arrival as soon as you can

- Before shaking hands with client, wipe your hands thoroughly with a dry handkerchief

- Never hand over a soiled, bent or creased visiting card

- Do not write anything on your brochure or visiting card. This creates an impression of lack of respect for your own organisational literature

- If you are meeting the client at a neutral venue, primarily check for client's comfort, convenience, preference of cuisine and choice of place

- If meeting is at a neutral venue, ask client if he would like to be picked up from somewhere

- Allow client to be seated at table first

- During meal, avoid ordering food with onion and garlic

- Do not order non-vegetarian food for yourself if client is a vegetarian

- Ask client what he prefers to order

- Be polite to waiters and service staff

- Don't complain about the food or the service, unless it is really poor

- Always offer to pay the bill
- When meeting ends, thank the client for his valuable time

Song of the
Super Salesperson

Song of The Super Salesperson

Ever onward, ever upward, your only goal is to reach the sky
Ever onward, ever upward, you can reach it if you try

Remember that Rome wasn't built in half a day
Work honest, work hard, and things will have to go your way

Do not merely fix your mind upon the quickness and the pace
It is always steady, sure and perfect, that wins the long race

Be happy, joyous, cheerful; always let your heart rejoice
Between a smile and a frown, by far the smile's the better choice

Wouldst you better your chance of selling, to your prospect you should be appealing
Improve your grooming, perfect grooming; this will make for better dealing

Gentle walking, gentle talking, make a perfect gentleman
None can then ever resist you, though he tries the best he can

Personalised service is what your customers would prefer, customised service is what your customers need
So let your customers do the talking, your job is to listen and do the deed

If you meet all your commitments, once you've given your valuable word
In the minds of your customers, you'll always be first, second and third

Punctuality is impressive, punctuality is the key
This simple rule is oft forgotten, but it leads from
'You' and 'I' to 'We'

Love what you're selling, that's important; that is something
you should do
Only if you love your product, will your prospect love it too

Learn all you can about your profession, you've chosen it to make your
life
Acquire all the knowledge that's possible, your career will then be free of
strife

But indifference is a killer, indifference you must shun
In a salesperson's mind this should be foremost, that away from
indifference you must run

Do that extra, little extra, always go the extra mile
In every business this is possible, it helps your business
run in style

It is said 'Knowledge is Power', this is also true for sales
Collect data, analyse data, this road to selling never fails

'Give more than you get', is life's great golden rule
If you've yet to learn that, then please go back to school

The strongest of us needs more than two hands to achieve
What ten average men can do, a giant may only conceive

There is no rule which exists that says 'only one can win'
In business and in life, putting down your rival is the only sin

'Sell anything to anyone?' in selling there can be no greater crime
If you proceed with this false motto, your career won't be worth a dime

A 'No' is sometimes said in anger, a 'No' is sometimes said in pain
Do not take it to heart and person; whistle, move on, try again

But should you try to be too pushy, folks away from you will run
Selling then is never easy, selling then is never fun

Feet be quick but mind be quicker, this will make order books thicker
With fast mind and faster wit, your sales career will be a hit

Your customers are many, they come in every shape and size
The salesperson who doesn't judge them, will walk off with the prize

Understanding your customer, is the single biggest thing
If this is what you're good at, soon you'll rise from Jack to King

Only of 'I', 'Me', 'Myself', alone; please do not ever think
At any cry or call for help, please do rush without a blink

Make a sale once, make a sale twice; after that you've made a friend
In your sales career that's important, that's what matters in the end

The 'Moment of Truth' is where all sales come from, the 'Moment of Truth' is of importance prime
In business, the 'Moment of Truth' is all encompassing; a great one helps you win each time

Others speaking on your behalf, will make your reputation soar
When others recommend your services, prospects trust you more and more

Joining, mixing, merging, mingling; will help you generate revenue
Network, network, always network; business opportunities will improve

Price comes later, price comes after, price is always secondary
First show value, genuine value, of what use you can be to me

Can your customers do without you? Don't be mistaken; yes they can
No one on earth is indispensable, but strive to be your customer's right hand man

Giving feedback to the management is part of every salesperson's task
Feedback from your customers, it is your job to ask

If you follow all our simple rules ten times out of ten
Then we're sure you'll never face real problems ever again

Brains Trust Management Consultancy

The motto of the consultancy says it all – **Invest In Intellect**

Founded and headed by two leading Indian management experts and best-selling authors, Brains Trust specialises in conducting branded training workshops which are based on the best-selling books of the founders, and also providing consultancy in core areas of management.

The focal attention of Brains Trust lies in providing practical and profitable consultancy solutions in the areas of:
> Strategy Formulation and Implementation
> Mystery Shopping
> System and Process Mapping and Re-engineering
> Customer Experience Mapping and Enhancement
> Organisational Communication

Highly acclaimed training workshops are conducted in the areas of:
> Sales Force Effectiveness
> High-level Communication Techniques
> Customer Experience Management
> Problem-Solving and Decision-Making
> Effective Leadership
> Six Sigma and Quality Practices
> Marketing Analytics

These words of **Mr. Roy Fonseca,** CEO - BASF Styrenics Pvt. Ltd. bear testimony to the credentials of Brains Trust:
"The expanse of their knowledge and the sensitivity with which they connect with all levels in their audience, make the training programmes conducted by Cyrus and Kalim extremely effective. Their training programmes are defined by a practical, well researched, hands-on approach, which keeps the participants engaged with the topic, not just during the training but long after."

Training Workshop on
Customer Experience Management
The 13 Tenets to Seal the Hole in the Bucket

This two day module is based on the best-selling work on Customer Service – **Seal the Hole in the Bucket**. This book is divided into two parts and deals with the Philosophy and Implementation of Customer Retention.

Part One, in which for the first time ever, the exact difference between the terms Customer and Consumer has been clearly defined. This is important, as the entire gamut of Customer Service and Retention is based on this vital difference. Part One also introduces the 'Brains Trust Customer Retention Model', which is essential to be understood for the process of Strategy Formulation. Part One ends with reinforcing the WHY of Customer Retention, i.e. the philosophy of WHY an organisation needs to focus the bulk of its resources on the vital area of Customer Retention, thus bringing an era of Marketing Renaissance.

Once the WHY of Retention has been clearly established, Part Two of this book then proceeds to explain the HOW of Customer Retention through 13 principles or tenets which form the heart and backbone of Customer Experience Management, an area in which the two authors (who will personally conduct the programme), are the acknowledged authorities in India.

These 13 Tenets do not require any financial investment or new technology, but actually save your organisation money by massively reducing advertising expenditure and replacing it with positive word of mouth publicity from delighted customers.

This programme is based on this book, as well as the other best selling work on Customer Service by the same authors – **Where is My Ketchup?**

Training Workshop on
Super Salesperson Skill Set

Introduction

This two day workshop is based on the best selling book – **Be A Super Salesperson**. The authors of this unique work have through immense research, both qualitative as well as quantitative, which has been conducted on all stakeholders involved in the process of selling, identified the attributes, characteristics and qualities which a salesperson in any industry needs to possess for sales success. These findings have been consolidated into 32 attributes, each unique but simultaneously dependent on the other. These 32 attributes have been composed into a song comprising of 32 stanzas, each stanza devoted to an individual attribute. This song is an anthem for salespersons to motivate themselves and develop and enhance these skills through excellent examples and inputs which have been provided for each stanza.

Module Content

The programme begins with a tribute to the profession of selling, which is the only function in an organisation which generates revenue. Once the participants have understood this key role that they play as revenue generators, the programme then goes on to explain and elaborate each of the 32 attributes in sequential order. The overall flow of the programme shall contain:
1. The Art and Science of Salesmanship
2. The Process of Selling
3. The Asset called – Salesperson
4. Inculcating the 32 essential attributes of a Super Salesperson
5. Self Motivation for Salespersons
6. Exhaustive Checklists for Fail-proof Selling

For workshop details, visit : www.brainstrustindia.com

226

About the Authors

CYRUS M. GONDA

An MBA in H.R. (Rank Holder) from NMIMS, Mumbai, Cyrus is a member of the prestigious International Society of individuals with Genius Level IQ - Mensa, a solid proof of his intellectual ability and creative process.

Currently the H.O.D. - Strategic Management with Rizvi Institutes of Management and also the Vice Principal of the National Institute of Event Management, he has also been a visiting faculty at JBIMS, NMIMS and other prestigious B-Schools.

Cyrus has conducted Corporate Training Programmes and Workshops on Customer Relations, Transactional Analysis, Japanese Management Techniques, Presentation Skills, Selling Skills, Time Management, Stress Management, Personality Development and related areas for reputed Organizations such as the Indian Navy, Godrej, BASF, VSNL, BARC, Mahindra & Mahindra, Indian Oil, Wockhardt and many other establishments, which have been highly appreciated by the participants.

Cyrus conducts System Audits and Kaizen and 5S Audits as well as implementation of the same for leading organisations such as Godrej, Della Tecnica (India's leading Architecture and Design firm), and other leading organizations.

He also wrote a regular column on the practical aspect of Human Resources and its relation to Customer Service in the 'Express Hotelier and Caterer'.

Cyrus is a voracious reader and has a fantastic eye for detail and a keen and inquiring mind, which help in identifying areas of improvement in Business Processes and Customer Service.

A great story teller with a wealth of anecdotes related to every subject, Logical Thinking and Analysis are his forte.

Dr. KALIM KHAN

Dr. Kalim Khan is currently the Director of Rizvi Institute of Management Studies & Research and is associated with the Institute for a decade now. It is due to his untiring and ceaseless efforts that the Institute has in a short span of time raised itself into the upper echelons of Management Institutes in the country. An academician by choice he entered the field of Management Education very early in his career. He is now a renowned brand in the field of Management Education and is especially known for his knowledge and expertise in the area of Quantitative Techniques and Marketing Research.

Dr. Kalim Khan is also one of the most sought after trainer in corporate India. He has been conducting regular training programmes in the areas of Customer Experience Management, Sales Force Management, Marketing Analytics, Problem Solving and Decision Making, Systems Management and Six Sigma.

Some of the companies for which successful programmes have been conducted are Godrej, TATA Communications, Della Tecnica, Philips, Colgate Palmolive, TATA Motors, Crompton Greaves, Mahindra & Mahindra, Airtel, Abbott BASF among others.

He is the co-author of two Best Selling Books on Customer Experience Management in the Indian context. Both these books "Where is My Ketchup?" and "Seal the Hole in the Bucket" written along with his faculty colleague Prof. Cyrus Gonda have received rich accolades from all quarters.

A firm believer in the concept of continuous improvement, he constantly upgrades his knowledge and skills in his areas of expertise. He is an avid reader and his reading range from Management to Fiction to his profound love for Urdu poetry.